This book belongs to:

_____

_____

FIVE-MINUTE
MINUTE
Bedtime
Stories

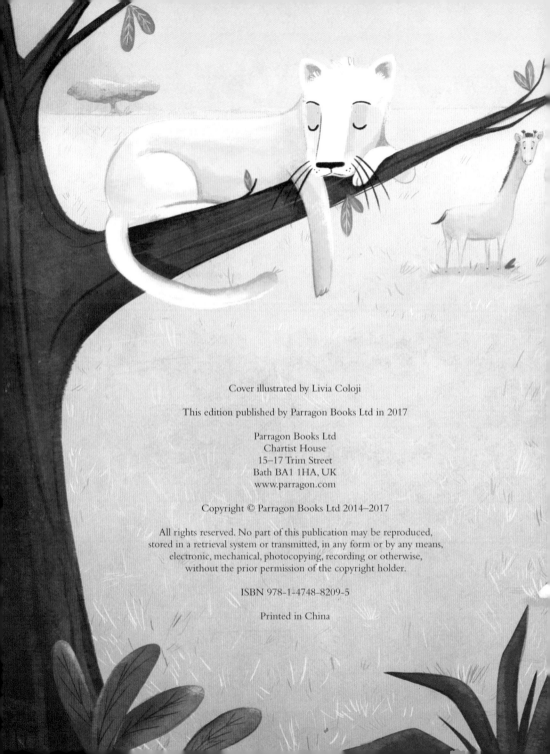

Cover illustrated by Livia Coloji

This edition published by Parragon Books Ltd in 2017

Parragon Books Ltd
Chartist House
15–17 Trim Street
Bath BA1 1HA, UK
www.parragon.com

ISBN 978-1-4748-8209-5

Printed in China

FIVE-MINUTE
Bedtime Stories

PaRragon

Bath · New York · Cologne · Melbourne · Delhi
Hong Kong · Shenzhen · Singapore

Contents

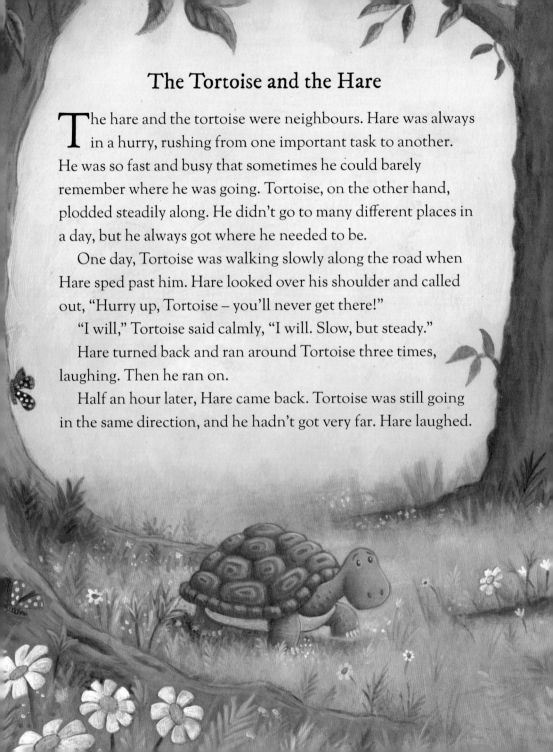

The Tortoise and the Hare

The hare and the tortoise were neighbours. Hare was always in a hurry, rushing from one important task to another. He was so fast and busy that sometimes he could barely remember where he was going. Tortoise, on the other hand, plodded steadily along. He didn't go to many different places in a day, but he always got where he needed to be.

One day, Tortoise was walking slowly along the road when Hare sped past him. Hare looked over his shoulder and called out, "Hurry up, Tortoise – you'll never get there!"

"I will," Tortoise said calmly, "I will. Slow, but steady."

Hare turned back and ran around Tortoise three times, laughing. Then he ran on.

Half an hour later, Hare came back. Tortoise was still going in the same direction, and he hadn't got very far. Hare laughed.

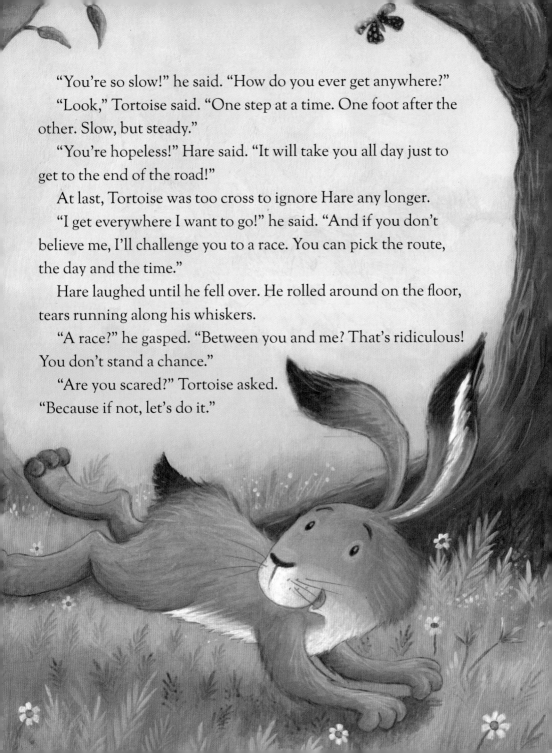

"You're so slow!" he said. "How do you ever get anywhere?"

"Look," Tortoise said. "One step at a time. One foot after the other. Slow, but steady."

"You're hopeless!" Hare said. "It will take you all day just to get to the end of the road!"

At last, Tortoise was too cross to ignore Hare any longer.

"I get everywhere I want to go!" he said. "And if you don't believe me, I'll challenge you to a race. You can pick the route, the day and the time."

Hare laughed until he fell over. He rolled around on the floor, tears running along his whiskers.

"A race?" he gasped. "Between you and me? That's ridiculous! You don't stand a chance."

"Are you scared?" Tortoise asked. "Because if not, let's do it."

Hare could hardly stop laughing, but they arranged the race for the next day and asked Fox to judge it. They would start from an old oak tree and race all the way to the river.

Tortoise set out early that evening so that he would be at the start line on time in the morning.

Hare went home for a long sleep and got up late. He ran to the oak tree and found Tortoise ready and waiting. All the other animals had come out to watch.

"Fox is waiting for you at the river," Bear said. "We can start whenever you're ready."

Hare and Tortoise got into position.

"On your marks," said Tortoise.

"Get set," said Hare.

"Go!" shouted all the animals.

Start

And off went the tortoise and the hare.

Hare sprinted ahead, bounding along the path. Tortoise lifted one foot, and put it down. Then he lifted the other foot, and put it down. Slowly, slowly. By the time Tortoise reached the first bush, Hare was a tiny spot in the distance. By the time he reached the second bush, Hare was nowhere to be seen.

After a few minutes, Hare could see the river ahead. He paused and looked around. He couldn't see Tortoise at all.

"He is so slow!" he laughed to himself. "He won't be here for hours. I might as well have a rest." So Hare sat down under a tree not far from the finish line. The sun was warm, and the lazy buzz of bees visiting the flowers around him was soothing. Soon Hare dozed off.

Back along the path, Tortoise carried on, slow but steady, one step at a time, one foot after the other.

To the river

After an hour, Hare woke up and peered into the distance. He could just see Tortoise coming towards him, slow but steady, and still far away.

"He's so slow!" Hare said to himself. "He won't be here for hours. I might as well go back to sleep." And that's just what he did.

Tortoise carried on, slow but steady, his heavy shell wobbling along the path. Hare slept on in the hot sun.

When Hare woke up, he couldn't see Tortoise anywhere.

Finis

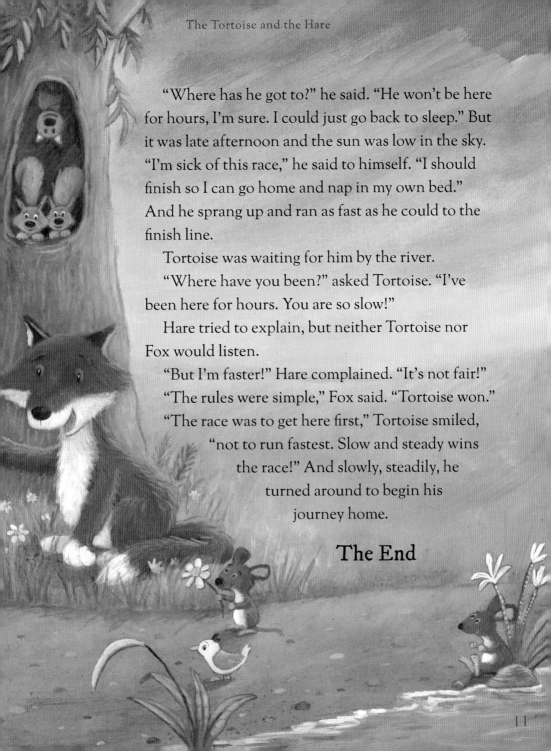

"Where has he got to?" he said. "He won't be here for hours, I'm sure. I could just go back to sleep." But it was late afternoon and the sun was low in the sky. "I'm sick of this race," he said to himself. "I should finish so I can go home and nap in my own bed." And he sprang up and ran as fast as he could to the finish line.

Tortoise was waiting for him by the river.

"Where have you been?" asked Tortoise. "I've been here for hours. You are so slow!"

Hare tried to explain, but neither Tortoise nor Fox would listen.

"But I'm faster!" Hare complained. "It's not fair!"

"The rules were simple," Fox said. "Tortoise won."

"The race was to get here first," Tortoise smiled, "not to run fastest. Slow and steady wins the race!" And slowly, steadily, he turned around to begin his journey home.

The End

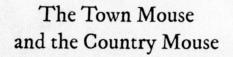

The Town Mouse
and the Country Mouse

Once upon a time, there were two little mice. One of them lived in the town, and the other one lived in the country.

One day, the Town Mouse went to visit the Country Mouse. He had never been to the country before so he was very excited. He packed a small suitcase and went on his way.

Country Mouse's home was small and dark – not at all like Town Mouse's home. Lunch was very different too. There was creamy cheese, juicy apples and crispy, crunchy hazelnuts. It was all very tasty, but when Town Mouse had finished, he was still hungry.

After lunch, Country Mouse took Town Mouse for a walk. They went down a sunny path, through a creaky gate and into a large field. Town Mouse was just starting to enjoy himself when...

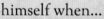

"Moo!"

"What was that?" he asked nervously,
scurrying closer to Country Mouse.

"Ha! That's just a cow," said his friend. "There are lots of them in
the country. It's nothing to be scared of."

Town Mouse and Country Mouse strolled on, through a flowery
meadow and over a grassy hill. Soon, they came to a peaceful pond.
Town Mouse was just starting to enjoy himself when...

"Hiss!"

"What was that?" he asked again, quivering from nose to tail.

"Ha! That's just a goose," said his friend. "There are lots of
them in the country. It's nothing to be scared of."

Town Mouse and Country Mouse carried on walking, across a rickety bridge, down a sandy track and into a shady wood. Town Mouse was just starting to enjoy himself when...

"Twit-twoo!"

"What was that?" he yelped, and he jumped off the ground in terror.

"It's an owl!" cried Country Mouse. "Run for your life! If it catches you, it will eat you up!"

So the two mice ran and ran until they found a leafy hedge to hide in.

Town Mouse was terrified. "I don't like the country at all!" he said. "Come to stay with me in the town. You'll see how much better it is!"

Country Mouse had never been to the town before, so he packed a small rucksack and went to stay with his friend.

Town Mouse's home was huge and grand, not at all like Country Mouse's home.

Lunch was very different too! Instead of apples and nuts, there were sandwiches and cupcakes and chocolates. Lots and lots of them. It was tasty, but soon Country Mouse began to feel a bit ill.

After dinner, the friends went out for a walk. They walked past shops and offices and houses. Country Mouse was just starting to enjoy himself when...

"Beep-beep!"

"What's that?" he asked fearfully, looking about him.

"That? It's just a car," said his friend. "There are lots of them in the town. It's nothing to be afraid of."

Then the mice walked through a park, past a church and down a wide road. Country Mouse was just starting to enjoy himself when...

"Nee-nah! Nee-nah!"

"What's that?" he asked again, his whiskers twitching.

"That? It's just a fire engine. There are lots of them in the town. It's nothing to be afraid of."

As the mice pitter-pattered home they passed a playground, a school and a pretty garden. Country Mouse was just starting to enjoy himself when...

"Meow!"

"What's that?" he squeaked, his eyes as wide as saucers.

"It's a cat!" cried Town Mouse. "Run for your life! If it catches you, it will eat you up!"

So the two mice ran and ran, all the way back to Town Mouse's home.

Country Mouse was terrified! "I don't like the town at all! I'm going home," he said.

"But how can you be happy living near the cow and the goose and that horrible owl?" said Town Mouse.

"They don't scare me!" cried Country Mouse. "How can you be happy living near the cars and the fire engines and that terrible cat?"

"They don't scare me!" cried Town Mouse.

The two mice looked at each other. Who was right and who was wrong? They would simply never agree. So they shook hands and went their separate ways: Town Mouse to his grand home and Country Mouse to his cosy one.

"Home, sweet home!" said the Town Mouse, sighing a deep, happy sigh.

"Home, sweet home!" said the Country Mouse, smiling a big, happy smile.

And the two of them lived happily ever after, each in his own way.

The End

The Dog and His Reflection

Puppy was having the best day of his life. The farmer had just given him his very first bone. It was a magnificent bone, with lots of juicy meat. Although Puppy couldn't wait to tuck in, he wanted to show it off around the farm first.

"What a fine bone," said Hen as Puppy strutted proudly past.

"It's nearly as big as you!" laughed Cow.

"Mmm, that looks tasty," said Fox. "You wouldn't like to share it, would you?"

Puppy quickly trotted off, the bone still clenched firmly in his teeth. He was looking for a place where he could be on his own, with no one else hungrily watching him. So he headed for the wood.

Puppy had never been into the wood before. It always looked very dark and scary but it seemed a good place to enjoy his bone in peace. But the wood was even scarier than he imagined. An owl hooted at him from the trees.

"Sorry, didn't mean to frighten you," said the owl. "I was just admiring your fine bone. Make sure you take good care of it."

Although the owl turned out to be friendly, Puppy still didn't really like the wood. So, he ran all the way through to the other side where he found lush green fields.

Puppy had never been this far away from home. It was exciting but a little scary too. Soon he came to a wooden bridge over a very clear river. This was very different from the streams around the farm which were all muddy and full of weeds. Puppy was curious.

On the other side of the bridge, a family of rabbits were playing in the field.

"The rabbits won't want to share my bone," Puppy thought. "I'll pop over the river and tuck into it in peace."

By now Puppy was feeling very hungry indeed. All he wanted was to sit in the soft grass and chew his bone in peace. He wobbled as he started crossing the old bridge. He tried not to look down but when he reached the middle, he could not resist a quick glance.

He was surprised to see another dog peeping out from under the bridge.

Puppy went a bit closer to the edge to have a better look. As he did so, the other dog peeped out even further so Puppy could now see his whole face. In between his teeth, he was also carrying a bone! And it looked just as big and juicy as Puppy's bone.

"I wish I could have that bone too," thought Puppy.

So, he started to growl at the other dog, hoping that it would make him drop the bone and run away.

Now the owl had flown out of the wood and come to perch on a nearby tree. He was watching Puppy very carefully.

"Oh dear," said the owl with a shake of his head.

Puppy began to growl even louder at the other dog. After all, that dog did not look any bigger than himself. But the other dog still refused to run off, seeming to growl back.

"It's not a real dog or a real bone," hooted the owl. "Be happy with what you already have instead of being greedy and trying to have even more."

But Puppy was not listening. He suddenly let out the fiercest bark he had ever made. **"Woof! Woof!"**

Immediately, the other dog dropped his bone.

Puppy felt very proud of himself. But then he realized that he didn't have his own bone either. It must have fallen out when he opened his mouth to bark. Yes, there it was – right at the bottom of the river!

Puppy sniffed miserably. He noticed that the other dog was sniffing miserably too.

It was then that Puppy finally realized that the other dog wasn't real at all. Nor was the bone. The owl was right. It was just himself, reflected in the clear water.

Seeing what had happened, one of the little rabbits hopped on to the bridge.

"Don't worry," he cried. "Come and play with us."

But Puppy did not feel like playing. Instead, feeling hungry and sad, he set off on his own.

Just as the wise owl had told him, he should have been content with the gift he had and not greedily wanted even more.

The End

Peter and the Wolf

Peter lived with his grandfather in a little cottage in the valley. Grandfather taught him to be kind to the animals and Peter soon became friends with many woodland creatures.

Grandfather also taught Peter about the dangers of living in the woods and how he must always be on the alert for wolves. Which is why Grandfather insisted that the cottage gate was kept closed.

Early one morning, Peter woke before Grandfather and as the sun was starting to rise above the mountains, he set off to play. Peter was so eager that he forgot to close the gate. He ran into the big green meadow. Seeing the gate wide open, the duck waddled through the yard and followed Peter.

Peter headed for his favourite tree where his friend, a little bird, was perched.

"Morning Peter," the bird chirped happily.

Peter climbed onto the lower branch and started chatting. Everywhere was so quiet, there wasn't even a ripple on the pond in the meadow.

Then suddenly they heard an excited **"Quack!"**

"Oh, no, I forgot to close the gate!" cried Peter. "Why did you follow me?" he asked the excited duck. "Grandfather is going to be so cross."

"Quack! Quack!" replied Duck, heading straight for the pond.

Now Duck and the little bird always found something to argue about. As Duck waddled along, the little bird joined him.

"What kind of a bird are you if you can't fly?" he chirped.

"And what kind of a bird are you if you can't swim?" replied the duck before diving into the pond with a big splash. And as the duck swam and the bird hopped along the side of the pond, they continued to argue.

Suddenly Peter noticed a cat ready to pounce on the bird.

"Look out!" cried Peter. And in a flash, the little bird was back in the tree again.

The cat stared in surprise as the duck flapped her wings wildly. Then the cat turned his attention to the bird once more and began to circle the tree. He wondered if he could climb up quickly enough to catch the little creature before it flew away again.

"It certainly isn't quiet any more," smiled Peter as he watched in amusement. But then an angry voice made him jump.

"Peter! Peter, how could you leave the gate open?" cried Grandfather, running across the meadow. "What if a wolf had come?"

"Boys like me are not afraid of wolves," replied Peter. But Grandfather did not want to hear this.

He led Peter across the meadow, and back to the cottage. As Peter waited behind the gate, he realized that Grandfather did know best. For at that moment, a big grey wolf appeared.

Seeing the little duck swimming on the pond, the wolf bared his teeth and licked his lips. The duck jumped out of the pond in fright at the sight of the wolf. And in no time, the wolf was chasing the little duck across the field. No matter how hard she ran, she couldn't escape from the wolf. Nearer and nearer came the wolf until **SNAP!** The duck disappeared.

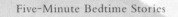

Quick as a flash, the cat climbed the tree. Soon the wolf began to circle, staring up with his greedy eyes. The cat stared back – he wasn't afraid. But the wolf was only interested in the little bird. He bared his teeth and snarled.

Watching in horror, Peter wasted no time. He grabbed some rope and made a lasso. He knew he couldn't let the wolf see him, so he carefully crawled towards his friends. Then he climbed the little wall beside the tree and called out, "Listen carefully, Bird, fly just above the wolf's head but take care he doesn't catch you."

The little bird did as he was told. As the wolf snapped, the bird swooped up and down, just out of reach. While the clever bird distracted the wolf, Peter leapt on to the tree.

He tied the end of the rope to a branch and dropped the lasso over the wolf's tail. The more the wolf jumped, the more the rope tightened around his tail. And the more angry he became.

Just then some hunters appeared, following the trail of the wolf.

"We've caught the wolf!" cried Peter. "Help us to take him to the zoo."

The hunters were happy to help. At the head of the group was Peter, followed by the hunters leading the wolf. Grandfather trailed along at the back, still cross with Peter for disobeying him.

"If Peter hadn't caught the wolf, what then?" grumbled Grandfather. He was not happy that Peter took such a risk.

"But Peter and I were too clever for the wolf," the little bird told Grandfather.

Now if you listened very carefully as the group passed by, you would just hear a faint **"Quack!"** The wolf was in such a hurry when he ate the duck that he swallowed the bird whole and the brave creature was still alive.

The End

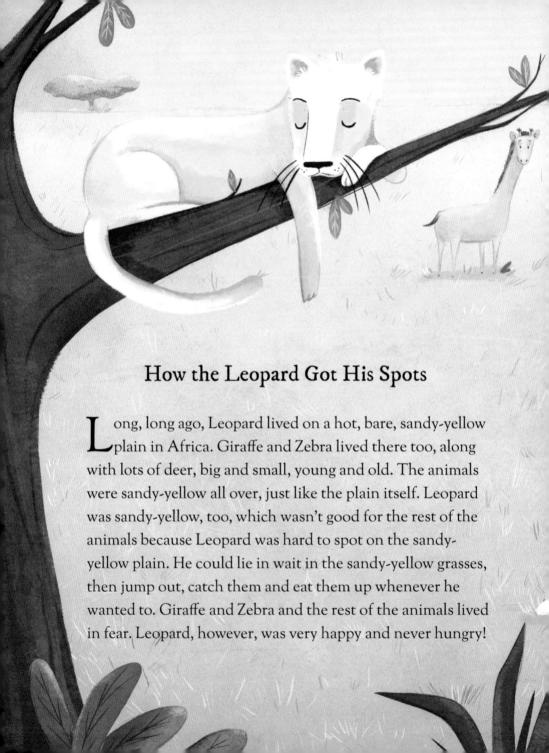

How the Leopard Got His Spots

Long, long ago, Leopard lived on a hot, bare, sandy-yellow plain in Africa. Giraffe and Zebra lived there too, along with lots of deer, big and small, young and old. The animals were sandy-yellow all over, just like the plain itself. Leopard was sandy-yellow, too, which wasn't good for the rest of the animals because Leopard was hard to spot on the sandy-yellow plain. He could lie in wait in the sandy-yellow grasses, then jump out, catch them and eat them up whenever he wanted to. Giraffe and Zebra and the rest of the animals lived in fear. Leopard, however, was very happy and never hungry!

After a while, Giraffe and Zebra and the others had had enough. They decided to move away from the sandy plain to find a better place to live. They walked and walked until they came to a huge forest where the sun shone through the trees making stripy, speckly, patchy shadows, and sections of spotty, stripy sunshine. The animals hid themselves there, and while they hid, partly in the sun, partly in the shadows, their skins changed colour. Giraffe's skin became covered with big, brown, blotchy spots from the blotchy shadow he stood in, and Zebra's skin became covered with stripes from the stripy shadow he lay in. The other animals' skin became darker, too, with wavy lines and patterns from the shadows around them.

Back on the sandy plain, Leopard was puzzled. All the animals had disappeared and he was starting to get hungry.

"Where have they all gone?" he asked Baboon.

"To the forest," said Baboon carelessly. "And they've changed. You need to change too."

Leopard started to ask Baboon what she meant by 'change', but Baby Baboon needed feeding, so she was too busy to explain.

Leopard set out for the forest. He walked and walked and at last he found it, but all he could see was tree trunks. They were speckled, spotted, dotted and splashed with shadows. He couldn't see Giraffe or Zebra or any of the others, but he could smell them so he knew they were there.

Leopard lay down to wait. After a long, long time, something moved in the shadows and a small deer trotted towards him. But sandy-yellow Leopard wasn't hidden in the leafy, green forest, so the deer saw him at once and skipped away. All Leopard could catch was its tail.

"I'm too small to fill your belly," cried the deer. "Please, let me go."

The deer was right about that. It was tiny and thin and not really worth bothering about, but Leopard kept hold of its tail anyway.

"What's happened to all the animals?" asked Leopard.

"We've all changed," the deer replied. "Now our skins are speckly, spotty, dotty and splashy, just like the shadows in the forest. You only caught me because I'm young. I should have been more careful."

Leopard let the little deer go and sat down to think. "So that's why I can't see Giraffe and Zebra and the rest of them in the forest," he thought. "They've changed their skins to match the shadowy trees. If I'm going to catch them, do I need to change too? And how in the world can I do that?"

As he sat there thinking, more deer walked through the trees. When they moved, Leopard could see them clearly. When they stopped moving, they were hidden by the shadows. Leopard was easy to spot with his sandy-yellow skin, so the deer didn't come too close.

Leopard sat in the shadows a long, long time and licked his paws thoughtfully. Soon he began to notice something odd. His paws weren't sandy-yellow any more. They had small, dark spots on them. And there were spots on his tail, too.

Leopard looked around and realized that the spots on his skin matched the small, dark patches of shadow he was lying in. "Ah-ha!" he thought. "The shadows have made these spots, just in the time that I've been lying here. That's how I can change my skin, just like Giraffe and Zebra and the rest of them!"

By this time, Leopard had grown tired from all the thinking and waiting, so he lay down and fell into a deep sleep. When he awoke a long, long time later, his skin was completely covered in small, dark spots, made by the shadows of the forest.

"Well, how wonderful!" he said, looking at his new skin. "Now my skin is no longer sandy-yellow-brownish, I can hide in the leafy, green forest so that Giraffe and Zebra and the rest of them can't see me. Then, when they come close, I can leap out to catch them and eat them up!"

With that, the spotty Leopard set off into the speckly, blotchy, stripy shade of the deep forest where he lived happily ever after, eating and sleeping and not being spotted. And the other animals learned to hide from him as best as they could, too!

The End

How the Rhinoceros Got His Skin

Long ago, among the tall trees near the shores of the Red Sea lived a very rude rhinoceros. He had no manners then and he has no manners now. You could recognise him by the horn on his nose but in those days his skin was smooth and tight and there wasn't a wrinkle in sight! He had three buttons on his tummy which made it look just like a well-fitted jacket.

One day as Rhinoceros was searching for food, a traveller arrived on the beach and decided to bake a cake in his little oven. He sang to himself as he mixed flour and water, and currants and plums and lots of sugar. Happy with his mixture, he popped it in the oven while he dozed under the burning sun. Soon the sweet smell of cake filled the air.

"Delicious!" smiled the traveller when the cake was ready.

In the nearby woods, Rhinoceros suddenly stopped in his tracks and lifted his head. He sniffed and sniffed.

"Cake!" he snorted as the warm smells wafted above his horn. Then he followed his nose and headed for the beach. When the polite traveller saw him coming he said, "Good morning," but the rude creature didn't even give a grunt.

Instead, he charged ahead, knocking the cake out of the traveller's hands. Then he spiked the cake with his horn, and lumbered back to his home. There he lay in the shade enjoying every crumb.

Meanwhile, the traveller climbed a palm tree and sat on high, thinking and planning.

"Just wait," he muttered, "I'll teach that rhino a lesson."

A few weeks later, when searing heat prompted everyone to take to the sea, the traveller knew the time had come. He was sitting on the beach wearing his hat to screen him from the ferocious sun when he spied Rhinoceros. His eyes followed the creature as he heaved his great body along the sand. Not noticing the traveller, Rhinoceros finally stopped.

Rhinoceros slowly undid his three buttons, took off his skin and carried it over his shoulder as he went down to the sea to bathe. Leaving his skin at the edge of the water, he waddled into the sea. The traveller immediately jumped up. He danced around the skin and rubbed his hands with glee.

"I'm ready!" the traveller cried. "Just you wait and see." Then he set off back to his camp.

As the traveller only ever ate cake, and rarely cleaned up, there were plenty of crumbs around his camp.

"Lots of crumbs! Crumbly crumbs!" he sang as he quickly filled his hat with the stale cake crumbs. Then he raced back to the beach.

Picking up the skin of the rhinoceros, the traveller sprinkled the inside with lots of dry, tickly cake and some baked currants. Then he left the skin for Rhinoceros, climbed to the top of his palm tree and waited.

Rhinoceros took his time in the sea. He lay on his back and blew bubbles through his nose. He splashed and splashed, never caring about others in the water. Finally, as his great big tummy started to rumble, and feeling much cooler from his swim, Rhinoceros returned to the beach.

Thinking about what he was going to eat, Rhinoceros picked up his skin and buttoned it up. No sooner had he finished closing the last button than the crumbs started to itch. He wriggled and wriggled. He began to scratch, but that made it worse.

"Ow! Ow!" he cried loudly.

Then he lay down on the sand and rolled and rolled and rolled but every time he rolled, the cake crumbs dug into him, making it more and more uncomfortable. He was beginning to feel very hot again and very, very cross.

He lumbered up to a palm tree and rubbed himself against the trunk but still the itching continued. He pressed his shoulders so hard against the tree that he rubbed his skin into a great fold. Then his legs started to itch so he rubbed them up and down the tree until folds appeared over both legs. He was now feeling very tired and as he pressed his itchy tummy against the tree, he rubbed off every button. Finally, a huge fold of skin appeared across his tummy.

The traveller looked down from the palm tree, watching his plan working. The rhinoceros became more and more bad-tempered as the cake crumbs continued to itch and scratch.

Feeling exhausted and very angry, Rhinoceros finally gave up and headed back home.

And from that day to this, every rhinoceros has great folds in his skin and a very bad temper, all because of the cake crumbs inside.

The End

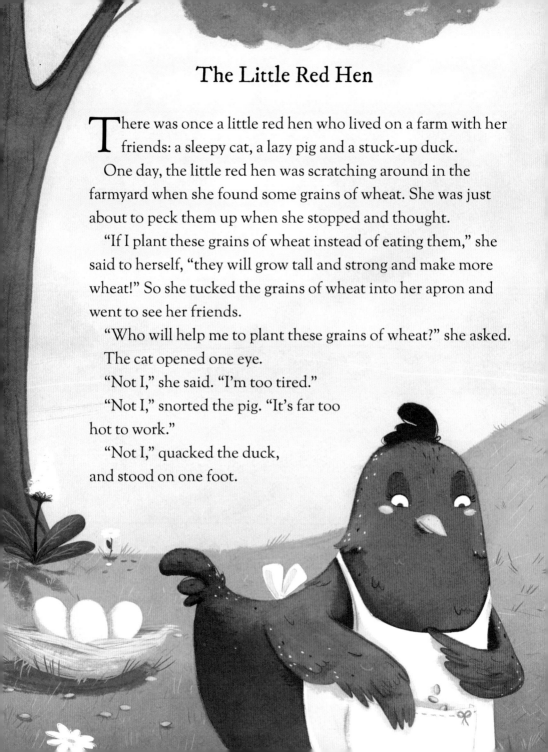

The Little Red Hen

There was once a little red hen who lived on a farm with her friends: a sleepy cat, a lazy pig and a stuck-up duck.

One day, the little red hen was scratching around in the farmyard when she found some grains of wheat. She was just about to peck them up when she stopped and thought.

"If I plant these grains of wheat instead of eating them," she said to herself, "they will grow tall and strong and make more wheat!" So she tucked the grains of wheat into her apron and went to see her friends.

"Who will help me to plant these grains of wheat?" she asked.

The cat opened one eye.

"Not I," she said. "I'm too tired."

"Not I," snorted the pig. "It's far too hot to work."

"Not I," quacked the duck, and stood on one foot.

So the little red hen found a patch of soil. She moved the stones and dug the earth. She made a row of holes and planted all the grains of wheat. Then she watered them carefully and left them to grow.

All summer, the sun shone on the grains of wheat and the rain fell on them. Each day, the little red hen checked they were not too dry or too wet. She pulled up the weeds and made sure the wheat had space to grow. At last, the wheat was strong and tall with fat, golden grains.

"This wheat is ready to harvest," she said to herself. "That will be a lot of work." The little red hen went to see her friends.

"I have worked all summer and the wheat is ready. Who will help me to harvest it?" she asked.

The cat stretched lazily.

"Not I," she said. "It's time for my nap."

"Not I," snorted the pig. "I need to roll in the mud."

"Not I," quacked the duck, and she preened her feathers.

So the little red hen took her tools and went to harvest the wheat. She cut down the wheat stalks and piled them up neatly. When she had finished, she went back to her friends.

"I have worked all day to cut down the wheat," she said. "Who will help me to make it ready for the mill?"

The cat yawned.

"Not I," she said. "I'm sleepy."

"Not I," snorted the pig. "I'm going to lie in the sun."

"Not I," quacked the duck, and tucked her head under her wing.

So the little red hen went back to the field alone. She beat the wheat to free the grains from the stalks, and carried away the straw. The wind blew, and the little red hen worked long and hard. At last, she swept up the wheat and put it into a sack. She carried it back to her friends.

"I have worked all day to prepare the wheat," she said. "Who will help me to carry it to the mill?"

"Not I," said the cat. "I need a rest."

"Not I," snorted the pig. "It looks far too heavy."

"Not I," quacked the duck, and she waddled away to the pond.

So the little red hen carried the heavy sack of wheat all the way to the mill. The kind miller ground the wheat to flour and poured it back into the sack. Then the little red hen carried it all the way home again.

The little red hen was exhausted.

"I have carried the wheat to the mill and had it ground to flour," she said. "Who will help me to bake it into bread?"

"Not I," said the cat, and she curled up, ready to sleep.

"Not I," snorted the pig. "It's nearly time for my dinner."

"Not I," quacked the duck, and she sat on the ground.

So the little red hen made the flour into dough and kneaded it. She shaped it into a loaf and put it in the oven to bake. After a while, a delicious smell wafted from the kitchen. The sleepy cat opened her eyes. The lazy pig came to stand by the oven. The stuck-up duck waddled in.

At last, the bread was cooked. The little red hen carried the loaf to the table. It had a beautiful golden crust on the top and was creamy white inside. It smelled wonderful.

"Who will help me to eat this loaf of bread?" the little red hen asked quietly.

"I will!" said the sleepy cat, washing her paws with her tongue.

"I will!" grunted the lazy pig, licking his lips.

"I will!" quacked the stuck-up duck, flapping her wings.

"No, you will not!" the little red hen said. "I planted the grains and watched them grow. I harvested the wheat and took it to the mill. I ground the flour and baked the bread. My chicks and I will eat the loaf!"

And that is what they did. The little red hen and her little chicks ate up every crumb of the hot, fresh bread.

The End

The Wolf in Sheep's Clothing

There was once a wolf who lived in a forest beside a sheep farm. You might think this would mean he would never be hungry, but there was a problem. Four sheepdogs guarded the large farm and the wolf was no match for all of them.

"I should be having lamb dinner every day," whined the lean, miserable wolf. His eyes narrowed hungrily and his long red tongue drooled as he spied on the sheep from the shadows of the forest. "Look how deliciously plump they are, feeding on that lush grass all day!"

The clever sheepdogs always made sure that one of them was awake right through the night. And if that dog so much as sniffed a wolf's scent in the air, he would bark at the top of his voice until the farmer came running out.

"Stay away from my sheep!" the farmer would yell as the wolf ran for his dear life back into the forest. "Come near my farm again and it will be the end of you!"

So as the sheep grew ever fatter, the wolf became hungrier and hungrier. He didn't know how he was going to survive. Then one day, as he peered longingly through the trees, he noticed that the farmer was shearing the sheep. He watched as the thick woolly coats disappeared, one by one.

"I'm taking these to market," the farmer told his sheepdogs as he lifted the coats on to the back of his truck. "You keep an eye on that wolf for me. Any sign of him, then teach him a lesson he'll never forget."

The wolf continued to watch from the safety of the trees as the farmer drove his truck out of the farm. Just as the truck was disappearing over a hill, the wolf saw one of the bundles of wool fall off the back and on to the road. With a sly grin, the wolf suddenly had a wicked idea. Using the cover of the trees and the hedges, he sneaked along the road until he reached the bundle. He quickly unrolled it and draped the thick sheep's coat over his head and back.

"Look at me, a poor sheep who has lost his way!" he practised his new voice. "I'd better go to that flock over there and see if they'll let me join them!"

Feeling very pleased with himself, the wolf made his way back towards the farm, being careful to keep his head near the ground.

"Baaa! Baaa!" he bleated as the four sheepdogs approached, wondering where he had come from. The wolf meekly told them his made-up story and then held his breath.

To his delight, the sheepdogs believed him and let him pass to join their flock. The sheep also believed him, taking great pity on the wolf and welcoming him right into their centre. It was just where the wolf wanted to be, well hidden from the dogs.

"Are you hungry?" one of the sheep asked the wolf kindly.

"Yes, I am a little," the wolf bleated meekly, thinking how tasty the sheep looked. "I haven't eaten for days."

"Well, there's lots of lush grass here," the sheep said kindly.

The sly wolf started to plan when to pounce. He allowed himself a little smile when one sheep told him about a wolf lurking in the forest.

"Don't worry," the sheep reassured him, "the sheepdogs won't let him get anywhere near."

His cunning plan had worked. The sheep were all fooled by his sheep's coat. All, that is, except the youngest. This small, scrawny lamb kept sniffing at the wolf. She was so new to the world that she did not know what a wolf was. But she knew what a sheep was.

"She smells different to us, Mama," the lamb bleated.

"Ah, that's probably because she's had a long, rough journey," Mother explained.

"And, look, she's got claws," the lamb said, so small that she could see right underneath the wolf's false coat. "And long sharp teeth!"

At the mention of teeth, the sheep all started to bleat very loudly. The deafening noise alerted the four sheepdogs who raced towards them. The wolf immediately broke free of the flock, his wool coat sliding off as he made desperately for the trees. The dogs were right on his heels, barking fiercely.

It was only when the wolf had reached his cave right in the middle of the forest that he knew he had escaped the dogs. But his body was still trembling from head to toe.

As for the sheep, they vowed to be a lot more careful in future. They would never foolishly trust a stranger again, whether he looked just like them or not.

The End

The Ant and the Grasshopper

Grasshopper loved the summer. He would spend all day perched on the blades of grass, basking under the sun. Just occasionally Grasshopper would hop from one blade to another but most of the time he was happy to do absolutely nothing.

Grasshopper idly rubbed his legs together, making a happy chirping sound. "Long summer days lazing in the lush green grass," he thought to himself with a smile. "Oh, can there be anything better!"

Grasshopper was just about to doze off when there was an annoying heaving and panting sound right beneath him. It was an ant pushing a piece of corn across the ground. No wonder he was panting because the corn was twice as big as he was and the nearest cornfield was a good distance away.

"What a silly thing to do on a hot sunny day like this!" Grasshopper laughed. "Just look at you – all hot and bothered!"

"It has to be done," said Ant, wiping his brow. "I have to take this corn to my nest."

"No, you don't," said Grasshopper. "You could just eat it here rather than drag it all that way. Come on, we'll have a picnic!"

Ant wiped his brow again. He would have loved to stop for a picnic but there was far too much work to be done. "You don't understand," he told Grasshopper. "This corn isn't to eat now. It's to store in my nest," he explained.

Grasshopper laughed so much that he nearly fell off his blade of grass.

"But that means you'll be going backwards and forwards, heaving heavy loads, from dawn to dusk," he mocked. "In all this heat!"

"I know," said Ant. "But it's so that I have plenty of food for winter. Nothing grows then. It's not like it is now, when there's food wherever you look."

Grasshopper lazily glanced all around him. It was true, there was food wherever you looked: lush grasses, golden fields of corn, delicious little fruits and berries. And it was also true that by winter it would have all disappeared. But that did not mean he was going to scurry frantically about like Ant, puffing and panting, on a hot sunny day.

"Winter's ages away," said Grasshopper. "Enjoy the lovely summer with me. Crawl up here and let's have that picnic."

However, Ant was already crawling away, lifting the ear of corn again, heaving it across the ground.

"Crazy!" Grasshopper called after him.

"We ants like to think ahead," Ant panted in reply, not for a moment pausing in his heavy task. "Summer won't last for ever."

Grasshopper jeeringly shook his head, reclining on his lush blade of grass. As he looked up at the perfect blue sky, he wondered how anyone could possibly think about winter on a day like this. It seemed to Grasshopper that summer would surely go on forever.

The summer lasted for weeks and weeks, months and months, but it did not go on forever. Eventually the long cloudless days became a little shorter. The sun was not quite so hot now, and the flowers were starting to fade. Autumn had arrived.

"I had better stock up with food," Grasshopper said to himself, climbing down from his blade of grass with a shiver. He was sure there would be a little bit left before the frost and snow arrived.

"Where can I find some food?" he asked a little mouse who was peeping out from the leaves.

"There's nothing growing," replied Mouse. "You're too late. Even the fruit that fell from the trees has all been carried away by the other animals."

Grasshopper was distraught. He felt so very hungry.

"How am I going to manage?" he asked the mouse sadly. He knew that when winter came, he would be starving.

Then he suddenly had an idea. He would visit Ant. With all that corn he had been storing up right through summer, Ant would surely have a little spare to give to his hungry friend.

By the time winter set in, the hunger and biting cold made Grasshopper weaker and weaker. It took him a long time to reach Ant's nest.

"Ant, are you there?" he called faintly. "It's your friend, Grasshopper. I've got no food. Could you spare me a little of yours?"

Ant took a good while to emerge from his nest. In fact, Grasshopper wondered whether he would appear at all. He remembered how unkind he had been to Ant in the summer.

Finally, though, Ant did emerge and he was carrying lots of food.

Grasshopper gobbled it all up gratefully. "I'm sorry I laughed at you for collecting all that corn," he said. "Next summer, I'll follow your example and think ahead!"

Ant smiled, pleased that Grasshopper had learned his lesson.

The End

The Lion and the Mouse

Once upon a time, there was a huge lion who lived in a dark, rocky den in the middle of the jungle. When the lion wasn't out hunting, he loved to curl up in his den and sleep. In fact, as his friends knew, if he didn't get enough sleep, the lion became extremely grumpy.

One day, while the lion lay sleeping as usual, a little mouse thought he'd take a short cut straight through the lion's den. The mouse lived with his family in a hollow at the bottom of a tall tree just on the other side of the lion's rocky home. He was on his way home for supper and didn't want to have to climb up and over the big boulders surrounding the den.

"What harm can it do?" he thought. "He's snoring so loudly, he'll never hear me."

As he hurried past the snoring beast, he accidentally ran over the lion's paw. With a mighty roar, the lion woke up and grabbed the little mouse in one quick motion.

"How dare you wake me up!" the lion roared angrily. "Don't you know who I am? I am King of the Beasts! No one disturbs my sleep. I will kill you and eat you for my supper." He opened his huge mouth wide.

Shaking with fear at the sight of all the lion's sharp, pointed teeth, the terrified little mouse begged the angry lion to let him go.

"Please, Your Majesty," he cried. "I didn't mean to wake you up. It was an accident. I was just trying to get home to my family. I'm too small to make a good meal for someone as mighty as you. Let me go and I promise to help you one day."

The grumpy lion stared at the little mouse. Then he laughed loudly.

"You help me?" he said scornfully, shaking his furry mane. "Ha! Ha! Ha! What a ridiculous idea! You're too small to help someone as big as me."

The little mouse trembled and closed his eyes as he waited for the terrible jaws to snap him up.

But to his surprise, the lion didn't eat him. Instead, the lion smiled and opened his paw.

"Go home, little mouse," said the lion. "You have made me laugh and put me in a good mood, so I will let you go. But hurry, before I change my mind."

The little mouse was very grateful. "Thank you, Your Majesty!" he squeaked. "I promise to be your friend forever, and I won't disturb you again."

As quickly as he could, the little mouse scurried home. What a story he would have to tell his children!

A few days later, the lion was out hunting in the jungle. As he crept stealthily through the lush undergrowth, he smelt something delicious. There, in a small clearing just ahead of him, stood a goat, eating the grass beneath a shady tree.

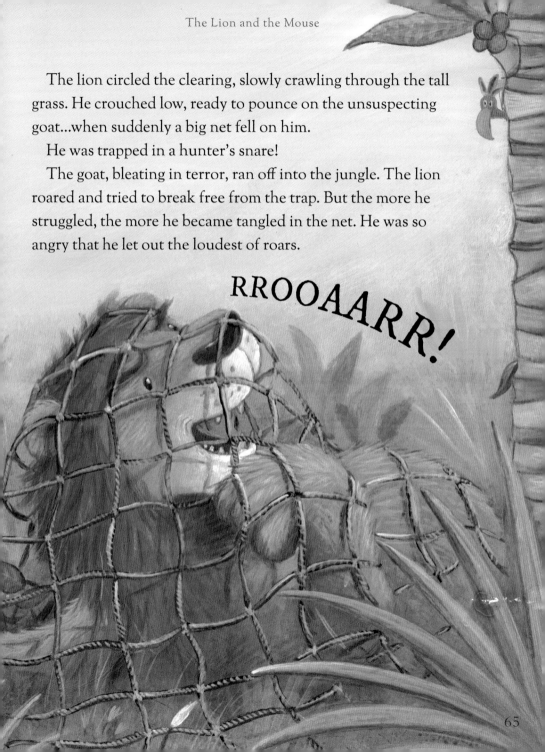

The lion circled the clearing, slowly crawling through the tall grass. He crouched low, ready to pounce on the unsuspecting goat...when suddenly a big net fell on him.

He was trapped in a hunter's snare!

The goat, bleating in terror, ran off into the jungle. The lion roared and tried to break free from the trap. But the more he struggled, the more he became tangled in the net. He was so angry that he let out the loudest of roars.

RROOAARR!

The trees in the jungle shook with the terrible noise. Every animal for miles heard it, including the little mouse.

"Oh no!" squeaked the mouse. "That's my friend, the lion. He must be in trouble! I've got to go and help him."

"Be careful, my dear," cried the mouse's wife. "Remember how big he is!"

The little mouse scurried through the jungle as fast as his tiny legs would carry him, towards the lion's mighty roar.

Soon he came upon the clearing and the lion, tangled and trapped in the ropes of the hunter's net.

"Keep still, Your Majesty," cried the mouse. "I'll have you out of there in no time."

"You?" laughed the lion.

The mouse ignored him and quickly started gnawing through the net with his sharp little teeth.

Before long, there was a big hole in the net, and the lion squeezed through the ropes and escaped his trap.

The lion held out his giant paw towards the little mouse. "Thank you, my little friend," he said humbly, bowing his huge head. "I was wrong when I laughed at you and said that someone as small as you couldn't help me. You saved my life today, and I am truly grateful."

The little mouse smiled up at the lion. "You were kind enough to let me go before, and I promised I would pay you back one day," he squeaked. "It was my turn to help you."

Side by side, the big lion and little mouse walked back into the jungle. From that day on the huge, mighty lion and the tiny, mighty mouse became the best of friends.

The End

How the Camel got his Hump

Long ago when the earth was still new, all the animals worked hard for their friend, Man. The horse carried Man on his back, the dog fetched wood for him and the ox ploughed the fields. But the lazy camel stayed in the desert and refused to do any work. He spent his time staring at his reflection in a pool of water, admiring his lovely slender neck and very long legs. The camel was always very unfriendly and only ever had one thing to say to the other animals: **"Humph!"**

One day, the horse rode deep into the desert and said to the camel, "Come out and trot with us."

"Humph!" replied the camel.

The next to approach the lazy creature was the dog. He came bounding up with a stick in his mouth. Excitedly, he dropped the stick and said, "Camel, come and fetch and carry like the rest of us."

"Humph!" came the reply as the camel continued to stare at his reflection.

When the ox heard how rude the camel had been, he decided to try. He trudged through the hot desert and finally reached the lazy camel.

"Come and help us to plough," he said.

But the only response was **"Humph!"** Camel was in no mood to talk to anyone.

At the end of the day, the Man called the three animals together.

"That lazy camel in the desert refuses to do any work," he said. "Now you will all have to work double time."

The three animals were very angry. They held a pow-wow to discuss what could be done.

"We can't go on working like this," complained the horse. And they all agreed.

Presently the Djinn of all Deserts appeared in a whoosh and a swoosh, rolling in a cloud of dust. Now the Djinn was a magic creature who always travelled that way. He was in charge of all deserts and was very wise.

"Oh, Djinn of all Deserts, is it right for anyone to be idle, with the world being so new?" asked the horse.

"Certainly not," replied the Djinn.

"Well," said the horse, "there's a thing in the middle of the desert with a long neck, long legs and a flat back. He hasn't done a stroke of work for three days."

"What does he say about it?" asked the Djinn.

"He only says, **'Humph!'**" said the dog. "And he won't fetch and carry."

"Does he say anything else?" asked the Djinn.

"No, and he refuses to plough," added the ox.

"Then I shall need to pay this lazy creature a visit," the Djinn of all Deserts told the three tired animals.

The very next day the camel was, as usual, admiring himself. Suddenly there was a whoosh and a swoosh and clouds of sand rose high into the air. Camel thought it was a sandstorm until the Djinn of all Deserts landed with a thump at his feet.

"Humph!" said the camel, although secretly he was very interested in the magical vision before him.

"What is all this I hear?" asked the Djinn. "Why are you not working, with the world being so new?"

"Humph!" replied the camel.

"You have given the horse, the dog and the ox a lot of extra work on account of your laziness. Aren't you a little sorry?"

"Humph!" came the same reply.

"Use that word once more and you will be sorry," warned the Djinn.

"Humph!" said the camel, but this was to be once too often.

The Djinn of all Deserts sat with his chin in his hand and began to work a great magic. Soon the perfectly flat back of the camel began to puff up and up into a great big lolloping humph.

"What has happened to my beautiful flat back?" cried the camel with huge salty tears falling onto the dry sand.

"Now you have your very own humph," the Djinn told him. "You brought this on yourself by your laziness." The camel was startled by this outburst. "Now you are going to put that humph to work," continued the Djinn.

"But how can I work with this huge humph on my back?" the camel quickly replied.

"It's the humph that will help you to work," the Djinn told him. "That humph will hold three days' food. You owe everyone three days' work so now you can work and not have to stop to eat."

The camel drooped his head sadly.

"And there will be no time to admire your reflection in the water," the Djinn of all Deserts added. And with a whoosh and a swoosh, he flew into the air.

And so the camel and his humph went to join the horse, the dog and the ox. And from that day to this, the camel always wears a humph (which we call hump now, not to hurt his feelings). But he has never yet caught up those three days that he missed at the beginning of the world, and he has never yet learned how to behave.

The End

The Peacock and the Crane

There was once a king in a far off land who had a magnificent palace. But his pride and joy were his stunning gardens, full of exotic trees and hedges, pretty fountains and quaint little mazes. Roaming around the palace gardens were graceful deer, while majestic swans and beautiful ducks drifted on its lakes.

But of all the animals that lived in the palace gardens, surely the most glorious was the king's peacock. Unfortunately, the peacock knew this too.

"Hello, deer," the peacock greeted them as he strutted across the grass, dragging his long tail feathers behind him.

"Hello, Peacock," the deer replied, knowing what question was going to come next.

"Who do you think is the most beautiful creature in the king's gardens?" the peacock asked, holding high his silvery blue neck and making his crown feathers stand up proudly on his head.

Now, the deer were themselves beautiful creatures, with huge eyes and pretty spots, but they simply could not compare to the peacock.

"You are the most beautiful, Peacock," the deer all replied humbly.

"Just as I thought!" said the peacock and he swept off to find another creature so he could ask exactly the same question.

The swans gliding gracefully across the lake were also very beautiful, with proud necks and pure white feathers gleaming in the sun. The same was true of the ducks. The king had specially chosen this exotic breed with orange tail feathers, and a lovely blush on their cheeks.

But, again, they could not compare to the peacock.

"You are the most beautiful, Peacock," the swans and ducks all admitted as the peacock asked the same question of each and every one of them.

Peacock smiled as he strutted around the palace gardens. How he loved to hear that answer. If any of the other animals hesitated for a moment, the peacock would quickly convince them by his favourite trick. He would suddenly raise his tail feathers to produce a huge, magnificent fan covered with shimmering blue and green spots. Faced with this stunning display, how could anyone deny that he was the most beautiful creature of all?

One day, Peacock noticed that the king had added a new animal to the palace gardens. It was a large wading bird, standing meekly at the edge of the lake. The peacock scoffed at the sight of this new arrival. It was the plainest creature he had ever seen, with dull grey feathers and lanky legs.

"What are you?" asked the peacock as he swept gracefully up to the grey newcomer.

"I'm a crane," the other replied.

"Is that so?" asked the peacock, rudely looking him up and down. "Are you proud of being a crane?"

"Oh yes," he replied confidently.

This annoyed Peacock. How could anyone looking as dull as that be so proud? Right away, the peacock asked his usual question.

"Who do you think is the most beautiful creature in the palace gardens?"

"Mm, I'm not sure," said the crane. "I haven't met everyone yet."

The peacock was more annoyed than ever. How was this dull creature likely to meet someone more beautiful than him? So, he did his usual trick – only this time he not only raised his tail feathers to produce a glorious blue and green fan, he also slowly turned this magnificent fan to the left and right.

"Now, who do you think is the most beautiful creature in the palace gardens?" the peacock taunted.

The crane was dazzled by the magnificent sight before him.

"It would surely be you," the crane said.

"At last! You've finally opened your eyes!" jeered the peacock.

"But beauty isn't everything," added the crane.

"What?" screeched the peacock in disbelief. "You mean, you don't want to look like me? You would rather be a plain, dull crane?"

"Yes, my feathers are rather plain and dull," the crane admitted. "But they serve me well, giving me a lot of pleasure." And to demonstrate, the crane opened his wings and took gracefully to the air. He flew all around the palace gardens, high above them.

"You see, your feathers might be beautiful," the crane called down, "but that's all they are, just for show. They can't make you fly and see all the wonderful things I can see."

The peacock enviously watched the crane circling high above, as happy as could be. That dull, grey bird was right: beauty isn't everything and there are a lot of other things that are important too. Peacock decided that he would never boast again.

The End

Chicken Licken

One day, Chicken Licken was walking along when an acorn fell from a tree and bounced off his head. The acorn rolled away before Chicken Licken knew what had hit him.

"Oh, my! Oh, dear!" he clucked. "Whatever shall I do?"

Chicken Licken flew into a panic. He ran around in circles in a flap, losing feathers as he went.

Along came Henny Penny.

"What's the matter?" she asked.

"THE SKY IS FALLING! THE SKY IS FALLING!" cried Chicken Licken, still in a panic.

Henny Penny was shocked. She did not know such a thing could happen.

"Cluck-a-cluck-cluck!" she shrieked. "We must tell the king at once!"

So Chicken Licken and Henny Penny rushed off to tell the king.

They flapped down the road, clucking as they went. Soon they met Cocky Locky.

"Where are you going in such a hurry?" he asked.

"THE SKY IS FALLING! THE SKY IS FALLING!" cried Chicken Licken.

"We're off to tell the king!" chattered Henny Penny.

Cocky Locky gasped. It would be terrible if the sky fell.

"Cock-a-doodle-doo," crowed Cocky Locky. "I'll come with you!"

So Chicken Licken, Henny Penny and Cocky Locky rushed off to tell the king.

They flapped and they flustered down the road, clucking and crowing as they went. Soon they met Ducky Lucky.

"Why are you flapping so?" she asked.

"THE SKY IS FALLING! THE SKY IS FALLING!" cried Chicken Licken.

"We're off to tell the king!" crowed Cocky Locky.

Ducky Lucky frowned. She didn't like the sound of that.

"How w-w-worrying," she quacked nervously. "I'm c-c-coming with you."

So Chicken Licken, Henny Penny, Cocky Locky and Ducky Lucky rushed off to tell the king.

They flapped and they flustered and they fidgeted down the road, clucking and crowing and quacking as they went. Soon they met Drakey Lakey.

"What's all the fuss about?" he asked.

"THE SKY IS FALLING! THE SKY IS FALLING!" cried Chicken Licken.

"We're off to tell the king!" quacked Ducky Lucky.

Drakey Lakey was dumbfounded. He dreaded the thought of a falling sky.

"Darn it!" he squawked. "I'll join you on your journey!"
So Chicken Licken, Henny Penny, Cocky Locky, Ducky
Lucky and Drakey Lakey rushed off to tell the king.

They flapped and they flustered and they fidgeted and they flurried down the road, clucking and crowing and quacking and squawking as they went. Soon they met Goosey Loosey.

"What's ruffled your feathers?" she asked.

"THE SKY IS FALLING! THE SKY IS FALLING!" cried Chicken Licken.

"We're off to tell the king!" squawked Drakey Lakey.

Goosey Loosey shuddered. Could it really be true?

"How horrible!" she honked. "I'm coming with you."

So Chicken Licken, Henny Penny, Cocky Locky, Ducky Lucky, Drakey Lakey and Goosey Loosey rushed off to tell the king.

They flapped and they flustered and they fidgeted and they flurried and they flopped down the road, clucking and crowing and quacking and squawking and honking as they went. Soon they met Turkey Lurkey.

"Where are you waddling to?" she asked.

"THE SKY IS FALLING! THE SKY IS FALLING!" cried Chicken Licken.

"We're off to tell the king!" honked Goosey Loosey.

Turkey Lurkey trembled. She thought that sounded truly terrible!

"My goodness!" she gobbled. "I'm coming with you!"

So Chicken Licken, Henny Penny, Cocky Locky, Ducky Lucky, Drakey Lakey, Goosey Loosey and Turkey Lurkey rushed off to tell the king.

They flapped and they flustered and they fidgeted and they flurried and they flopped and they floundered down the road, clucking and crowing and quacking and squawking and honking and gobbling as they went. Soon they met Foxy Loxy.

"Well, hello!" he said. "Why are you all in such a tizzy?"

"THE SKY IS FALLING! THE SKY IS FALLING!" cried Chicken Licken.

"We're off to tell the king!" gobbled Turkey Lurkey.

Foxy Loxy smiled slyly. He had never seen so many plump birds in such a fearsome flap.

"Well I never," soothed Foxy Loxy. "Don't worry, I know the quickest way to reach the king. Follow me."

So Chicken Licken, Henny Penny, Cocky Locky, Ducky Lucky, Drakey Lakey, Goosey Loosey and Turkey Lurkey followed Foxy Loxy down a long path and into some dark woods.

"Not far to go now," said Foxy Loxy.

They lumbered over logs and they lolloped over leaves until they found themselves at...Foxy Loxy's den!

Foxy Loxy and all his family licked their lips.

"Run!" cried Chicken Licken.

"Fly!" shrieked Henny Penny.

"Hurry!" honked Goosey Loosey.

And Chicken Licken, Henny Penny, Cocky Locky, Ducky Lucky, Drakey Lakey, Goosey Loosey and Turkey Lurkey ran as fast as their legs could carry them.

They flapped and they flustered and they fidgeted and they flurried and they flopped and they floundered right out of the woods and back up the long path, clucking and crowing and quacking and squawking and honking and gobbling as they went.

And they never did tell the king about the sky falling.

The End

Jack and the Beanstalk

Once upon a time, there was a young boy called Jack, who lived with his mother in a cottage. They were so poor that, bit by bit, they had to sell everything they owned just to buy their food. Then one day, Jack's mother said to him,

"We will have to sell Bluebell, our old cow. Take her to the market, Jack, and remember to sell her for a good price."

So Jack took Bluebell off to market. He had just reached the edge of the town when an old man appeared at the side of the road.

"Are you going to sell that fine cow?" said the man.

"Yes," said Jack.

"Well, I'll buy her from you, and I'll give you these magic beans," said the man, holding out a handful of dry beans. "They don't look much, but if you plant them, you and your mother will be rich beyond your wildest dreams."

Jack liked the sound of being rich. And he didn't even stop to wonder how this stranger knew about his mother!

"It's a deal!" he said. He gave Bluebell to the man and took the beans.

When Jack showed his mother the beans, she was so angry that her face turned as red as a beetroot!

"You stupid boy! Go to your room!" she cried, and threw the beans out of the window.

Jack sat on his bed, feeling miserable. "Stupid beans," he muttered. "Stupid me!" Then he fell asleep.

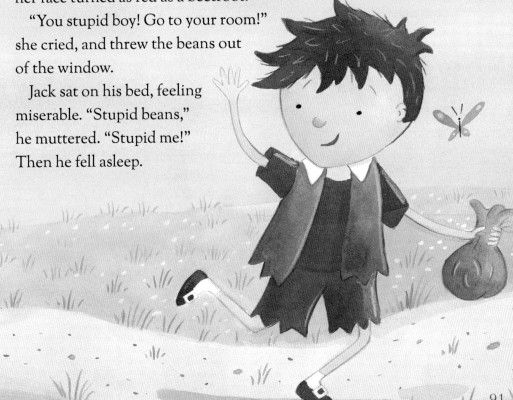

When Jack woke up
the next morning, it was
strangely dark in his room
and all he could see through
the window were the leaves of a
huge plant. A plant so tall that he
couldn't see the top of it.

"It must be a magic beanstalk!" cried Jack.
"What's at the top?"

So Jack started to
climb. Up he went, from
branch to branch and from
leaf to leaf. At the top was a
giant house. Jack's tummy was
rumbling with hunger, so he
knocked on the great big door.
A giant woman answered.

"Please, madam, may I have
some breakfast?" Jack asked politely.

"You'll become breakfast if my
husband finds you!" said the giant's
wife. But Jack begged and pleaded
and at last she let him in and gave
him some bread and milk.

The giant's wife had just shown
Jack where to hide when the giant
came home in a bad mood.

"Fee, fi, fo, fum, I smell the blood of an Englishman!" roared the giant.

"Silly man," said his wife. "You smell the sausages I have cooked you for breakfast."

The giant ate a giant-sized breakfast, then settled down to count the huge gold coins in his treasure chest. There were lots of coins. "One hundred and one...one hundred and two..." he counted, but his head started to nod and before long he was fast asleep.

Quick as a flash, Jack grabbed two of the huge gold coins and ran out through the front door. He raced to the beanstalk and climbed down it as fast as his legs would carry him.

His mother was so happy to see the gold that she hugged Jack for ten whole minutes!

"Clever boy, Jack!" she laughed. "We'll never be poor again!"

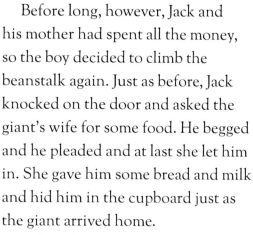

Before long, however, Jack and his mother had spent all the money, so the boy decided to climb the beanstalk again. Just as before, Jack knocked on the door and asked the giant's wife for some food. He begged and he pleaded and at last she let him in. She gave him some bread and milk and hid him in the cupboard just as the giant arrived home.

When the giant had eaten a giant-sized lunch, his wife brought him his pet hen. **"Lay!"** he bellowed, and the hen laid a solid gold egg. It laid ten eggs before the giant started to snore. Jack could hardly believe his luck! Quick as a flash, he picked up the hen and ran.

When his mother saw the hen lay a golden egg, she hugged Jack for twenty whole minutes!

Although Jack and his mother were now rich beyond their wildest dreams, the boy couldn't help himself – he decided to climb the beanstalk one more time.

This time, Jack knew that the giant's wife would not be happy to see him, so he sneaked in when she wasn't looking and quickly hid in the cupboard. The giant came home as usual and ate a giant-sized dinner, then his wife brought him his magic harp.

"Play!" he roared, and the harp began to play. It was such sweet music that the giant fell asleep in record time!

Jack grabbed the harp and started to run, but the harp cried out, "Master! Help!"

The giant woke up at once and chased after Jack. The boy slithered down the beanstalk faster than he'd ever done before, but the giant was catching up!

"Mother, fetch me the axe!" Jack yelled as he reached the ground. Then he chopped at the beanstalk with all his might.

Creak! Groan! The giant quickly climbed back up to the top just before the beanstalk crashed to the ground. When his mother heard the harp play, she hugged Jack for a whole hour! And, as you can imagine, the two of them lived happily ever after.

The End

The Cat That Walked by Himself

At the very beginning of time, wild animals lived in the Wet Wild Woods and the wildest of all was the Cat. He walked by himself, waving his wild tail.

One night, Wild Dog asked Cat to go with him to the cave where Man and Woman lived. But the Cat replied, "I am the Cat who walks by himself, and all places are alike to me."

As Wild Dog set off, Wild Cat was curious, and so he followed him, taking care not to be seen.

When he reached the cave, Wild Dog said to the Woman, "What is this that smells so good?"

And the Woman threw him a lamb bone. It was so delicious he begged for another. So the Woman said, "Help my Man to hunt through the day and guard this cave at night, and I will give you as many roast bones as you need."

Later, when the Man saw the Dog, the Woman said, "Take him with you when you go hunting as he is our friend."

Wild Cat was listening all the time and thought, "This is a very wise Woman, but she is not so wise as I am."

The next day the Wild Horse asked Wild Cat to help him search for Wild Dog. Now the Cat was keen to see what had happened to Wild Dog but because he didn't want Wild Horse to know this, he replied, "I am the Cat who walks by himself."

So Wild Horse set off alone, not realising that the Cat was following him.

When the Woman saw the Wild Horse, she laughed. "Wild Thing, you did not come here for Wild Dog, but for the sake of this dried grass." And then she promised him lots of wonderful grass if he wore a harness on his wild head.

And later she told the Man, "This Servant will carry us from place to place. Ride on his back when you go hunting."

Hearing this, the Wild Cat was even more impressed with how clever the Woman was.

It was Wild Cow's turn to visit the cave next. Wild Cow promised milk every day in return for the lush green grass. So the Woman agreed and later explained to the Man that the cow would provide food for them.

Listening once again, the Cat decided he should talk to the Woman himself.

So the next day, Cat visited the Woman and told her, "I am not a friend, and I am not a servant. I am the Cat who walks by himself, and I wish to come into your cave."

The clever Woman bargained with him, "I will give you warm milk three times a day for always but only if you do three things to earn my praise."

And the Cat replied, "The Curtain, the Fire and the Milk-pots will see that you keep your promise." Then the Cat returned alone to the Wild Wood.

Some time later, the Cat heard there was a baby in the cave.

"Ah," he said, "my time has come."

When he reached the cave, the Woman was busy spinning and the Baby was crying. The Cat patted the Baby with his paw, and he cooed; then he tickled him under his fat chin with his tail. And the Baby laughed.

Not seeing the Cat, the Woman was relieved that some creature had stopped her Baby crying. "What a gentle Thing!" she said.

Now the Curtain heard the Woman's praise and immediately fell down. When she found the Wild Cat underneath the Curtain, the Woman was very angry and sent the Cat away.

Later as the Baby started to cry again, the Cat crept back in and whispered, "I will show you a magic trick." Then he tied some thread to a piece of wood and chased it across the floor. The Baby laughed as much as he had been crying.

"Clever Cat," said the woman gratefully.

The fire heard the Woman praise the Cat and gave a great puff! The Woman was not pleased to see the Cat now sitting comfortably by her fireside. But when a little mouse ran across the floor, she jumped up on the footstool, quivering, until the Cat chased the mouse away.

"Thank you," she said. "You were very quick."

Now this was the third time the Woman had praised the Cat and the Milk-pot remembered her promise to provide the cat with milk. So the Milk-pot cracked in two and soon the Cat was lapping up the warm milk.

That evening, the Man also made
a bargain with the Cat.
"You can stay only if you catch mice in
the cave. If you fail, I will throw you out
the cave and so shall all Men."
Then the Dog bargained with the cat too.
"If you are not kind to the Baby I will chase
you up a tree. And so shall all dogs after me."
And so the Cat keeps his side of the
bargain, for as long as the Baby doesn't pull
his tail too hard. He will kill mice and be
kind to the Baby when he is in the house.
But between times, and when night comes,
he is the Cat that walks by himself,
and all places are alike to him.

The End

The Boy Who Cried Wolf

Once upon a time, there was a boy called Peter who lived in a little village in the mountains with his parents, who were sheep farmers. It was Peter's job to watch over the flock and protect the sheep from wolves.

Day after day, Peter sat on the mountainside watching the flock. It was very quiet with no one but sheep for company. No wolves ever came to eat the sheep.

Peter got very bored. He tried to amuse himself by climbing rocks and trees or by crawling through the grass and counting the sheep, one by one.

"One, two, three...sixty-four, sixty-five..." counted Peter, "Oh, I wish something exciting would happen. I'm so bored! Same old mountain, same old sheep..."

Finally, one day, Peter couldn't stand being bored any more. "I know what to do!" he grinned to himself.

He started shouting at the top of his voice, "Wolf! Help! Wolf!"

Down in the village, a man heard Peter's cries.

"Quick!" he shouted to some other men. "We need to help Peter. There's a big wolf attacking the sheep."

The villagers grabbed their axes, forks, shovels and brooms and ran up the mountain to where Peter was shepherding his flock.

When they got there, puffing and panting, all was quiet and the sheep were grazing peacefully.

"Where's the wolf?" one of the villagers cried.

Peter roared with laughter. "There's no wolf. I was just playing!"

The men were very angry with Peter. "You mustn't cry wolf when there isn't one," they said.

That night Peter got a telling-off from his mother and was sent to bed without any supper.

For a while after this, Peter managed to behave himself. He climbed the mountainside with the sheep every day and watched over them quietly. The villagers soon forgot about his trick.

Then one day, Peter got really bored again. He had already run up and down the rocks, climbed three trees and counted the sheep ten times.

"What can I do now? Same old mountain, same old sheep..." he groaned to himself.

With a sigh, he slumped to the ground. As he was sitting there, an idea popped into his head. He picked up some sticks lying nearby and started banging them hard together. Then at the top of his voice, he shouted, "Wolf! Help! Wolf! Please hurry, there's a big wolf eating the sheep!"

Down in the village, a crowd of people started gathering when they heard the loud banging and shouting coming from the mountainside.

"What's all that noise?" someone cried.

"It's Peter. He's in trouble!" shouted someone else. "Quick, there must be a wolf on the prowl."

Once again, the villagers grabbed their forks, shovels and brooms. They ran up the mountain to chase away the wolf and save poor Peter and his sheep.

And once again, when they got there, puffing
and out of breath, all was quiet and the sheep were
grazing peacefully.

"Peter, what's happened?" shouted one man angrily.

"There's no wolf," laughed Peter. "I was only playing."

"You shouldn't make jokes like that," said another man.
"It's not good to lie." The villagers marched back down the
mountain towards the village.

That night, Peter got an even bigger telling-off from his
mother and once again had to go to bed without
any supper.

For a few days, the villagers
went around moaning about
Peter and his tricks. But after a
while the incident was forgotten, and Peter
continued to climb the mountainside every day
with the sheep.

He had decided that he would try and behave
himself, especially as he didn't want another scolding
from his mother.

A few weeks later, while Peter stood counting the sheep as
usual to pass the time, he noticed that some of them were bleating
nervously. He climbed up a tree to take a look around and see
what was upsetting them.

To his horror, he saw a big hairy wolf. The terrifying
creature was creeping through the grass towards the
flock with its jaws open and its long
tongue hanging out. Peter could
see the wolf's sharp
pointed teeth.

Shaking with fear he started screaming, "Wolf! Help! Wolf! Please hurry, there's a big wolf about to eat the sheep!"

A few people down in the village heard his cries for help, but they carried on about their business as usual. "It's only Peter playing another trick," they said to each other. "Does he think he can fool us again?"

And so nobody went to Peter's rescue.

By nightfall, when Peter hadn't returned, his parents became concerned. Peter never missed his supper – something bad must have happened.

Peter's father gathered the people of the village, and together they hurried up the mountain, carrying flaming torches.

A terrible sight met their eyes. All the sheep were gone! There really had been a wolf this time.

Peter was still in the tree, shaking and crying.

"I cried out wolf! Why didn't you come?" he wept.

"Nobody believes a liar, even when he's speaking the truth," said Peter's father, helping him climb out of the tree. Peter hung on to his father all the way home. He never wanted to see another wolf ever again.

And Peter finally really learnt his lesson. He never told a lie again, and he always got to eat his supper.

The End

The Fox and the Crow

Most crows would accept that they are not the most striking birds. However, there was one crow who always sulked when the other woodland birds chatted about who was the most colourful or who had the finest voice. So she was not happy when a baby bird suddenly chirped, "Who has the most beautiful feathers?"

Before anyone could say a word, the crow answered, "The crow, of course."

Now the other birds laughed so much, the branches all swayed.

"Nonsense, everyone knows the kingfisher has the most beautiful orange and blue feathers," said the sparrow. "A crow is just the same dull colour from head to toe. Even the blackbird has orange feet."

"Well, who can sing the best then?" asked the baby bird.

And without hesitation the crow replied confidently, "The crow, of course."

This time some of the birds were knocked out of the tree, which shook from the laughter of all the birds.

"No, no!" chuckled the woodpecker. "It's the nightingale who has the sweetest song. A crow's voice is too croaky and makes me think of winter."

The crow was so upset, she wanted to fly off to be on her own. She hung her head in shame but then suddenly spied a large piece of cheese lying in the grass below.

"I do have a good voice," she told herself, "and I'm clever. None of the others have spotted that cheese." And she swooped down, grabbing the cheese with her sharp beak.

Then she flew back to the tree, flapping her wings proudly, showing off her prize to the envy of all the other birds.

"What a lovely piece of cheese," cried the sparrow. "Can we share it?"

But the crow shook her head. After all, why should she share when everyone had been so mean to her? So the other birds all flew away in disgust.

"Good," thought the crow, "now I can enjoy my cheese in peace." She flew up to a higher branch and settled herself.

But just at that moment, a beautiful red fox sauntered by. Spotting the crow, his eyes narrowed as he saw the cheese wedged in her beak.

"Mm, mm," thought the fox, "that looks a tasty piece of cheese, indeed. I must have it." Now the fox knew he needed a clever plan. So he slowly circled the tree twice before deciding what to do.

Seeing the fox, a family of rabbits quickly ran from the wood and into the meadow to hide. They knew exactly how dangerous he could be.

"Good morning," said the fox in his friendliest voice, calling up to the crow. "What a very fine bird you are! Look at your glossy feathers, how they shine. You must be the finest bird I have ever seen." And noticing the crow raising her head up high, he added, "None of the other birds in the wood is a match for you."

This is just what the crow needed to hear. No one had ever told her she had beautiful feathers. In fact no one had ever admired anything about her before.

"I am beautiful, too," she said to herself as she brimmed with pride.

The fox had hoped the crow would open her mouth to say thank you. So far, his plan was not working. He needed to think quickly.

"I imagine a bird with fine sleek feathers like you would also have a beautiful voice," he continued, using all his cunning.

The delighted crow nodded. "At last," she thought, "here is someone who appreciates me. All those other birds who think I have a croaky voice are plain wrong! I wish they could hear what this fox is telling me."

The fox was losing patience but tried once more.

"Would you be so kind as to share your beautiful voice with me?" he asked meekly. "I'm sure it's even sweeter than the song of the nightingale."

And this time the crow couldn't resist the fox's flattery.

"I do have a beautiful voice," she told herself. "And I'm going to prove it," she added defiantly. She puffed up her chest and opened her sharp beak.

"Caw! Caw! C–!" she croaked.

Down! Down! Down fell the cheese. Right into the fox's wide-open mouth. **SNAP!** went his jaws. The fox chewed the cheese very slowly, determined to enjoy every little bite. This was surely the best cheese he had ever tasted.

"So good!" he called up to the stunned crow. And as he slinked away he added, "You really are a very vain bird. A very vain bird who can't sing either."

As the crow sat on the branch all alone, she realized she had learned a very important lesson today. And she knew she would never be fooled by flattery ever again.

The End

The Sorcerer's Apprentice

Once upon a time, a young boy called Franz went to work as an apprentice for a sorcerer. The sorcerer lived in a huge castle overlooking the little village where Franz lived with his family. It was considered a great honour to help and learn from such a clever and powerful man.

Franz was very excited about learning how to do magic. But when he arrived on his first day, he was just given a long list of chores to do around the castle – cleaning, tidying up and fetching water from the well.

Franz was not happy. "It's not fair!" he muttered to himself. "I didn't come here to be his servant. When will I get to do some magic?"

The sorcerer was a busy man. Each morning he would tell his apprentice what chores needed doing that day. He would then disappear into his workshop in the castle or journey out to one of the surrounding villages in the area, leaving Franz alone.

Occasionally, as Franz went about the castle doing his chores, he would catch a glimpse of the great sorcerer looking through the pages of a large leather-bound book, which he kept locked in a wooden cabinet in his workshop. The pages of this book were filled with beautiful illustrations and the words of the sorcerer's magic spells. Franz longed to have a look in the book himself.

Several months later,
fed up with just doing chores
all day, Franz decided he would
sneak a look in the sorcerer's
special spell book when the old
man was gone.

As the sorcerer got ready to
leave the castle that day, he
called out to Franz.

"Boy, I need you to scrub the
floor of the Great Hall for me,"
he said. "You will need to fetch
water from the well with this
bucket, and carry it to the big
stone container in the hall."

Franz rolled his eyes behind
the sorcerer's back. "Of course,
sir," he mumbled.

"When the container is full of
water," continued the sorcerer,
"take the broom and give the
floor a good scrub. I want to see
it shining when I get back
this afternoon."

As soon as the sorcerer left, Franz climbed the small staircase to the workshop. He knew where the sorcerer kept the key to the wooden cabinet, so he grabbed it and hurriedly opened the old, creaking doors. Inside, on a shelf, sat the magic spell book.

Franz carried the heavy book to the Great Hall and sat down to look through its magical pages. There were spells for all sorts of weird and wonderful things.

As he turned the pages, Franz saw a spell that could bring any object to life. This gave him a brilliant idea.

"What harm can one little spell do?" he thought to himself.

Grinning, Franz rushed to fetch the broom and bucket. He placed the broom on the floor, sat back down at the desk and slowly chanted the words of the magic spell. He couldn't wait to see the broom clean the Great Hall by itself!

At first nothing happened. Franz was just about to try the spell again, when suddenly the broom sprouted little arms and leapt up from the floor. Franz was so surprised he nearly fell off his chair!

This was amazing. He was doing magic!

"Broom!" he commanded. "Take the bucket to the well and fetch water to fill that container."

The broom marched off to the well and started carrying the bucket backwards and forwards between the well and the container in the Great Hall.

Franz couldn't believe his eyes. Laughing as the little broom kept bringing the water, he cried, "I am the master! And you must obey me!"

After a while, Franz noticed that the container was overflowing and that the water was running all over the floor.

"Stop, little broom!" he shouted. The broom, however, carried on fetching water.

"What am I to do now?" thought Franz. Flipping through the pages of the magic book, he tried to find a spell to make the broom stop.

But the broom kept on going. By now the water was all over the floor. Franz grabbed an axe and chopped the broom into small pieces.

"That should do it," he said with a sigh of relief.

To his dismay, the little pieces of broom started to move and grow, and they too sprouted arms and legs. Soon there was an army of new brooms. They all began to march to the well to fetch more water.

Franz didn't know what to do! The brooms continued splashing the water into the Great Hall and soon it was swirling around Franz's knees. He was powerless to stop the brooms.

Just then, the sorcerer returned. He raised his arms and in a booming voice, chanted a magic spell. In an instant the brooms all vanished and the water disappeared. Everything returned to normal.

Shaking with fear, Franz fell to his knees. "Please forgive me, master," he begged. "I just wanted to try some magic."

The sorcerer was very angry. "Never play with things you don't understand!" he shouted. "Magic is very powerful and should only be used by a sorcerer."

Franz hung his head in shame. He would never get the chance to learn magic now.

"I should send you away, boy," continued the sorcerer, but he could see that Franz was very sorry. He decided to give him another chance.

"You can stay," he said. "You still have much training to complete."

Franz was so relieved. "Thank you, sir!" he said. "I promise I will work very hard."

"Well," said the sorcerer, "you can start by cleaning this floor – the old-fashioned way!"

The End

The Gingerbread Man

Once upon a time, a little old woman and a little old man lived by themselves in a little old cottage. One day the little old woman decided to bake a treat for the little old man.

"I'll make him a special gingerbread man," she thought.

She mixed all the ingredients together, rolled out the dough, cut out the gingerbread man and popped him in the oven to bake.

Soon a delicious smell filled the little old cottage.

The little old woman was just putting on her oven gloves to check her baking, when she heard a strange voice calling out.

124

"Let me out! I've finished baking and it's hot in here!"

The little old woman looked around. She was confused. "I must be hearing voices!" she chuckled to herself.

She opened the oven door and nearly fell over in surprise when the little gingerbread man jumped up off the baking tray, rushed past her and ran out through the front door.

"Come back," cried the little old woman. "You smell delicious. We want to eat you!"

But the gingerbread man was too fast for the little old woman. He ran into the garden and past the little old man.

"Stop!" cried the little old man, setting down his wheelbarrow. "I want to eat you!"

But the little gingerbread man was already halfway down the road outside the little old cottage. He was very fast, and the little old woman and the little old man were very slow.

"Stop! Stop!" they wheezed, out of breath, as they ran down the road.

The gingerbread man darted under a fence into a field, singing as he went:

"Run, run, as fast as you can,
You can't catch me, I'm the gingerbread man!"

As the gingerbread man ran through the field, he passed a pig.

"Stop!" snorted the pig. "I want to eat you!"

"I've run away from a little old woman and a little old man, and I can run away from you," he said.

And he ran even faster, followed by the little old woman, the little old man and the pig.

Soon the little gingerbread man met a cow.

"You smell scrumptious!" mooed the cow. "Stop, little man, I want to eat you!"

But the gingerbread man just ran faster. "I've run away from a little old woman, a little old man and a pig, and I can run away from you," he cried.

The cow started to run after the gingerbread man, but he sprinted past her through the tall grass in the field, singing out:

**"Run, run, as fast as you can,
You can't catch me, I'm the gingerbread man!"**

The little old woman, the little old man, the pig and the cow ran and ran, but none of them could catch the little gingerbread man.

In the next field, the gingerbread man met a horse.

"You look yummy!" neighed the horse. "Stop, little man, I want to eat you!"

But the gingerbread man just ran faster. "I have run away from a little old woman, a little old man, a pig and a cow, and I can run away from you!" he cried.

The horse started to gallop after the gingerbread man, but he was already halfway across the field. He turned and waved at the horse as he sang out:

**"Run, run, as fast as you can,
You can't catch me, I'm the gingerbread man!"**

The little old woman, the little old man, the pig, the cow and the horse ran, but none of them could catch the little gingerbread man.

The little gingerbread man squeezed through a hedge and ran on, faster and faster, along a path through a shady wood. He grinned, feeling very pleased with himself, and rather proud of how fast he could run.

"No one can catch me!" he giggled.

But just a little further on down the woodland path, the gingerbread man came to an abrupt stop. There before him flowed a wide river, completely blocking his way.

While the little gingerbread man was wondering how he was going to get across the river, a sly old fox came up to him.

"Hello, little man," said the fox, licking his lips. "You look like you could do with some help."

"Oh, yes please," cried the gingerbread man. "I've run away from a little old woman, a little old man, a pig, a cow and a horse, and I need to get across this river so that I can keep on running. And I can't swim!"

"Well, jump on my back, and I'll carry you across the river," grinned the sly old fox. "You'll be safe and dry."

So the little gingerbread man climbed onto the fox's tail and the fox began to swim across the river.

After a while, the fox said, "You're too heavy for my tail. Jump onto my back."

The little gingerbread man ran lightly down the fox's tail and jumped onto his back, clinging tightly onto his fur.

Soon, the fox said, "You're too heavy for my back. Jump onto my nose."

The little gingerbread man did as he was told and jumped onto the fox's nose.

At last, they reached the other side of the river. The gingerbread man was just about to jump to the ground when the hungry fox threw back his head. The little gingerbread man suddenly found himself tossed high in the air.

Then down fell the gingerbread man and **SNAP!** went the mouth of the sly old fox.

And that was the end of the little gingerbread man!

The End

Beauty and the Beast

There was once a rich merchant who had three daughters. The youngest daughter had a kind heart, unlike her jealous sisters. She was called Beauty.

Everything changed one winter when the merchant lost all his money and was forced to move into a little cottage. The two elder daughters wept in anger fearing no one would marry them now. They would stay in bed all day while Beauty rose at four each morning and cleaned the cottage and cooked their meals.

One day, the merchant received good news. One of his ships had been found, which meant he would have money again. He immediately set off for town.

"Bring me back a velvet cape," demanded the eldest sister.

"And I'll have a silk gown," added the second sister.

"What about you, Beauty?" asked her father kindly.

"Please bring me a rose, Father," said Beauty politely.

Beauty worried terribly about her father and longed for his safe return but she knew her sisters would tease her mercilessly if she said this.

Sadly the merchant had been given the wrong information. It was not his ship that had been found after all. With a heavy heart, he rode back, failing to notice the snow falling so thickly. Soon he was lost. He wandered for hours and when night fell, he began to despair. At last he spotted a golden light coming from a great castle.

Pushing on the open door, he found himself inside a dining hall where a fire blazed and a table was laid for one person. But there was no one to greet him. At last he said to himself, "I can wait no longer. Surely the kind master will pardon me if I eat alone."

After a good night's sleep, the merchant set off. Wending his way through a scented rose garden, he was reminded of Beauty's request. As he broke off a single red rose there was a thunderous roar and a hideous creature appeared before him.

"So this is how you repay my kindness!" snarled the creature. "I saved your life but you choose to steal the thing I love most. You deserve to die."

"Forgive me, Lord," begged the merchant. "I only wanted to pluck a rose for my youngest daughter."

"Call me Beast," snapped the creature. "I will spare your life if one of your daughters comes to stay with me of her own free will. But if none of them agrees, you must return within three months."

With a sad heart, the merchant agreed.

On hearing her
father's story, Beauty persuaded
him to take her to the Beast's castle.

When she arrived, she could hardly dare look at the creature.
But Beauty very soon came to realize that he had a good heart.

One evening as he joined her for supper, the Beast asked her,
"Do you find me ugly?"

And for the first time Beauty looked at his face.

"Yes, but you are very kind," she replied honestly.

The Beast seemed pleased by her answer and suddenly asked if
she would be his wife.

"No, Beast," she replied simply. And the Beast let out a
painful cry.

As the time passed, Beauty came to enjoy her life at the castle. She had everything she needed. As a sign of his love for her, the Beast gave Beauty a magic mirror to show her what was happening at home.

One day as she looked into the mirror, she saw her father was ill.

"I must go to my father," she told the Beast. "If you let me leave, I promise I will return."

Heartened by these words, the Beast agreed. "Take your mirror with you," he said. "And remember, if you do not return in one week, I shall die of grief."

Beauty's father was overjoyed to see her and he soon became well again. The foolish sisters had both married, but were unhappy. So they tricked Beauty into staying longer than the week. One day when Beauty was looking in her magic mirror, she saw the Beast was ill. She knew she had to return.

Arriving back at the castle, she found him close to death.

"You broke your promise," the Beast whispered, "and now I must die."

"No! No!" cried Beauty in anguish. And at that moment she knew she loved him.

"I want to be your wife," she pleaded. And as her tears fell on the Beast's face, a bright light dazzled her. Suddenly, standing before her was the most handsome man she had ever set eyes on.

"Where is the Beast?" she cried.

"I was your Beast," smiled the young man. "By choosing to stay with me and promising to be my wife, you have broken the spell."

Beauty and her Prince were soon married and lived happily in their castle.

The End

Dick Whittington and His Cat

Long ago there was a young orphan boy called Dick Whittington who loved to hear tales about the great city of London.

"Are the streets truly paved with gold?" he would ask, and the villagers always told him they were. So one day he decided to set off to make his fortune in London.

But as he entered the city, he found no gold. All day, he trudged through the narrow, grey streets and met people dressed in tattered clothes. Cold and hungry, Dick lay down on a doorstep and fell fast asleep.

He was woken abruptly by the bad-tempered cook of the house.

"Wake up you lazy boy," she said, prodding him, "you can't sleep here." Fortunately, Mr Fitzwarren, a rich merchant who owned the house, took pity on the poor boy.

"Give the lad some breakfast," he told the cook. "He can work in the kitchen and sleep at the top of the house."

The cook was not pleased. She made the boy clean pots, tend the fire and sweep the floor all day long.

Dick soon settled in, though, and the only thing he didn't like were the rats crawling all over his bed at night. So he saved up and bought himself a big cat.

In no time the cat had scared away all the rats and she and Dick became great friends.

One day as he was busy peeling potatoes, a young girl in a beautiful silk dress appeared at the kitchen door. It was Alice, the merchant's daughter. Dick had never seen anyone looking so clean and tidy. She told Dick that her father's ship was setting sail for Africa and it was the custom for all the servants to give the Captain of the ship a gift for good luck.

"All I have is my cat," said Dick sadly.

"Well you will just have to give that cat then," said the cook unkindly.

So the next morning Dick reluctantly handed over his cat. The cook teased him mercilessly about the cat. Dick became so unhappy, he decided to run away.

"London is not for me," he told himself.

Shortly after leaving the city behind, Dick stopped for a rest. As he sat beside a milestone, he suddenly caught the sound of the church bells. They seemed to be saying:

Turn again Whittington, Lord Mayor of London!

Dick leapt up as the pealing bells continued to ring out. He knew they were sending him a message.

"Me? Lord Mayor of London?" cried Dick. He picked up his knapsack and turned around. Then he headed straight back to the merchant's house in London.

LONDON
10 miles

Meanwhile Dick's cat had sailed all the way to
Africa. The ship was met by the King who was excited
to see all the fine things brought from London. He
promised the Captain gold in return for the goods
and invited him to his luxurious palace for a feast.

The Captain had never seen such splendour but soon he noticed that the palace had a problem. Rats and mice were running around freely, eating all the food.

"I think I can help you," the Captain told the King and the next day he returned with Dick's cat. Immediately, the cat sprang into action and in minutes all the rats and mice had scampered away.

The King had never seen a cat before and was delighted!

"I shall give you five hundred pieces of gold for this magnificent creature," he told the Captain.

"But if we set sail without the cat, the ship will be overrun with rats," the Captain told him. "They will eat all our food and we will starve to death."

"A thousand pieces!" cried the King.

"The cat is yours!" replied the Captain, hoping that this was a risk worth taking.

The Captain was lucky and the ship returned safely to London with all the gold. When Mr Fitzwarren heard the Captain's tale, he immediately summoned Dick and told him the happy news.

"Congratulations, Mr Whittington," he addressed Dick politely. "This gold is payment for your cat. You are a very rich man now."

And as Dick left the room, the words of the bells were in his ear:

Turn again Whittington, Lord Mayor of London!

"Maybe one day," he said to himself before setting off to buy all the servants a present. He even bought the bad-tempered cook a silver brooch. And for himself he bought fine clothes suitable for the gentleman he had now become.

Alice Fitzwarren thought he looked very handsome indeed and soon they became sweethearts.

When Dick told Alice about the message of the bells, Alice said, "I do believe that will happen."

And she was right! Some years after Dick and Alice were married, he did indeed become Mayor of London. And occasionally, he would travel out to the milestone in his gold carriage, driven by eight beautiful white horses. There he would think about his cat and remember the first time he heard the message of the pealing bells:

Turn again Whittington, Lord Mayor of London!

The End

LONDON
10 miles

The Goose that Laid the Golden Egg

There was a farmer and his wife who worked very hard but never had much to eat. The crops did not grow as well as on other farms and their animals never seemed to fatten up. You could see the bones on the cows and even the pigs were scrawny.

So, every day in the morning the poor couple had just a little bit of bread and a couple of glasses of thin milk. For dinner they had just the one goose egg between them. Indeed, their goose egg dinner was their only treat of the day. If there was a morning when the goose failed to lay an egg, they had to go without dinner that evening. But, fortunately, this rarely happened.

"She's a good goose," the farmer told his wife as he cut his half of egg into thin slices. That way it went further. The goose eggs were always delicious, firm and white on the outside and rich and yellow on the inside.

"Yes," the wife agreed. "She's a very good goose, even though we can't afford to feed her much."

There were times when the farmer and his wife envied the other farmers who had all sorts of fine foods for their dinner.

"If I were rich," said the farmer, "I would have roast beef every day."

"And if I were rich," said the wife, "I would throw away my old clothes and buy myself a beautiful new dress."

Of course, they both knew this was never likely to happen and they expected to be poor until the end of their days.

Yet one morning, as the wife put her hand in the hay to collect the goose egg, her heart nearly stopped. The egg felt particularly hard and shiny. She immediately thought something was wrong with the goose.

A few moments later, she was excitedly running across the fields in search of her husband.

"Come quickly!" she cried. "The goose has laid a golden egg!"

"That can't be true," the farmer said when she had at last found him. Then she showed him the golden egg. The delighted farmer lifted his wife into the air and they danced around the kitchen.

The couple wasted no time in making the long walk into town
to check that the egg really was made of gold. An old jeweller paid
them a very handsome price for it and so the wife was able to buy the
beautiful dress she had always dreamed of. They returned home in a
fine horse and carriage!

The next morning, they were delighted to see that the goose had
laid another golden egg. And it laid another the day after that. In
fact, it seemed that the goose could only lay golden eggs now.

"We must do everything we can to look after the goose," the wife said. "We need to make its cage much stronger so foxes or thieves don't take it. When word gets round about our goose that lays golden eggs, lots of people will try to steal it!"

They had the money now to look after the goose properly and they built the strongest, grandest cage imaginable. They also fed it the very best corn and bought it the finest hay to lay its special eggs on. All this attention worked because the goose continued to lay golden eggs day after day. And the farmer and his wife became richer and richer.

In spite of this, they started to wonder how to make even more money.

"Maybe if we fed the goose twice as much corn," the farmer suggested, "then it would lay two eggs a day instead of just one."

Sure enough, after giving the goose the extra corn, the next morning there were two shiny golden eggs lying in the cage. So they fed the goose three times as much corn a day, then four times. The more it was fed, the more golden eggs it laid.

But one morning they woke to find the goose writhing in pain, lying in the corner of the cage.

"We've overfed it!" the wife wailed. "Oh, why were we so greedy! Why couldn't we be content with just one golden egg a day?"

They did everything they could to revive the goose, nursing it day and night.

Finally, one morning the goose rose shakily to its feet. It was well again. It even laid an egg. But it was just an ordinary egg, not a golden one. In fact, the goose never laid another golden egg. And the farmer and his wife were never greedy again. They were just happy with what they had.

The End

Aladdin

Once upon a time, a boy called Aladdin lived with his mother. They were so poor that every day it was a struggle to find enough money for food.

One day a man came to their shack saying he was Aladdin's long-lost uncle. When he said he would help Aladdin to make his fortune, Aladdin and his mother were delighted.

Aladdin travelled with him into the desert until they came to a rock. The man pushed it aside, revealing a hidden cave.

"You must climb down into this cave and fetch a lamp that you will find there," he said. "Bring it to me. Don't touch anything except the lamp. Wear this magic ring to protect you."

Aladdin was afraid, but he dared not argue with his uncle. He put on the magic ring and climbed into the cave. As soon as he was through the entrance his eyes grew wide with wonder. All around, piles of gold and jewels stretched from floor to ceiling. Gemstones glittered in the dim light. Just one ruby would make Aladdin and his mother rich. But he did as he had promised and touched nothing. At last he found a dull, brass lamp.

"Surely this can't be it?" Aladdin thought, but he took it back to his uncle. When he got to the opening, he found he couldn't climb out of the cave holding the lamp.

"Pass it to me," his uncle said, "then I will help you out."

"Help me out first, uncle," Aladdin replied, "and then I will give you the lamp."

"No!" the man shouted. "First give me the lamp!"

When Aladdin refused, the man became angry. He rolled the stone over the opening to the cave, trapping Aladdin in the dark.

"Uncle!" Aladdin shouted. "Let me out!"

"Hah!" the man shouted back. "I'm not your uncle, fool! I'm a sorcerer! You can stay there and die, if you won't give me the lamp!"

Aladdin wrung his hands in despair. As he did so, he rubbed the magic ring the sorcerer had given him for protection. Suddenly, a genie sprang out.

"I am the genie of the ring. What do you require, oh master?" The genie bowed. Aladdin was astonished, but he thought quickly.

"Please take me home to my mother," he said. And immediately he was outside his mother's house. He told her everything that had happened, and she hugged him with relief.

"Oh, but Aladdin," she cried, "we are still poor!"

The next day, Aladdin looked at the lamp he had fetched from the cave. "It doesn't look like much," he thought, and he started to polish it, hoping he could sell it to get money for food. As soon as he rubbed the lamp, another genie appeared.

"I am the genie of the lamp. What do you require, oh lord?" the genie asked. This time, Aladdin knew what to do. He asked the genie to bring food and money so that he and his mother could live in comfort.

Life went on happily, until one day Aladdin saw the beautiful daughter of the emperor. He fell in love and felt that he couldn't live without her. But how could he marry a princess?

Aladdin thought and thought, and finally he had an idea. He asked the genie for beautiful gifts to give to the princess.

When the princess spoke to Aladdin to thank him for the gifts, she fell in love with him. They were married, and Aladdin asked the genie to build them a beautiful palace.

Hearing that a wealthy stranger had married the princess, the sorcerer guessed that Aladdin must have escaped from the cave with the lamp.

One day, when Aladdin was out, the sorcerer disguised himself as a poor tradesman. He stood outside the palace calling out, "New lamps for old! New lamps for old!"

Aladdin's wife remembered the ugly brass lamp that Aladdin kept and took it to the man. The sorcerer snatched it from her, rubbed the lamp and commanded the genie to carry the palace and the princess far away to his own home in another country.

"Where is my beautiful wife?" cried Aladdin when he returned home, wringing his hands in despair. As he did so, he rubbed the ring and the first genie appeared.

"What do you require, master?" the genie of the ring asked.

"Please bring back my wife and palace!" Aladdin pleaded. But the genie of the ring was less powerful than the genie of the lamp.

"Then take me to her so that I can win her back!" Aladdin said.

At once, he found himself in a strange city, but outside his own palace. Through a window he saw his wife crying, and the sorcerer sleeping. Furious, Aladdin climbed in through a window and crept to the bedroom. He slipped the magic lamp from beneath the sorcerer's pillow and rubbed it.

"What do you require, master?" asked the genie.

"Take us straight back home," Aladdin said. "And shut this sorcerer in the cave for a thousand years – that will teach him a lesson!"

In a moment, the palace was back where it belonged. With the sorcerer gone, Aladdin and the princess were safe again. They lived long and happy lives together and never needed to call on the genie again.

The End

Goldilocks and the Three Bears

Once upon a time, there was a little girl called Goldilocks, who had beautiful golden hair. She lived in a pretty house right at the edge of the forest. Each morning she liked to play outside before breakfast, gathering flowers and looking at the animals who lived in the trees.

One day she strayed further than usual. She skipped happily along the forest path, chasing butterflies, until she was far from home and very hungry.

Just as she was thinking that it would take a long time to walk back for breakfast, a delicious smell wafted through the woods. She followed it all the way to a little cottage.

"I wonder who lives here," Goldilocks said to herself. "Perhaps they would share their breakfast with me?" She knocked on the door, but there was no answer.

As Goldilocks pushed gently on the door, it swung open. The house inside was cosy and inviting. Even though she knew she shouldn't, Goldilocks stepped inside.

The delicious smell was coming from three bowls of steaming porridge on the table. There was a great big bowl, a middle-sized bowl and a teeny-tiny bowl. Goldilocks was so hungry that – even though she knew she shouldn't – she tasted the porridge in the biggest bowl.

"Ew!" she cried. "This porridge is too hot!"

Next, she tasted the porridge in the middle-sized bowl. "Yuk!" she said. "This porridge is far too cold!"

So finally she tried the porridge in the teeny-tiny bowl.

"Yum!" Goldilocks said. "This porridge is just right!" And she ate it all up.

With her tummy nice and full, Goldilocks decided to have a rest before she set out for home. She looked around the room for somewhere to sit. There were three chairs – a great big chair, a middle-sized chair and a teeny-tiny chair.

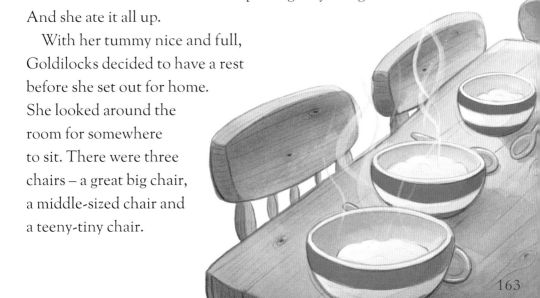

She climbed onto the great big chair.

"This chair is far too high," she said.

Next, she tried the middle-sized chair, but she sank deep into the cushions.

"No," she said, "this chair is far too squashy."

So she sat on the teeny-tiny chair.

"This chair is just right!" she said, settling down. But Goldilocks was very full of porridge, and too heavy for the teeny-tiny chair. It squeaked and creaked. It creaked and cracked. Then...

Crash!

It broke into teeny-tiny pieces, and Goldilocks fell to the floor.

"Well, that wasn't a very good chair!" she said crossly. Then, even though she knew she shouldn't, she went to look upstairs.

In the bedroom were three beds. A great big bed, a middle-sized bed and a teeny-tiny bed.

She tried to lie down on the great big bed, but it wasn't at all comfy.

"This bed is too hard and lumpy," she grumbled. Then Goldilocks lay down on the middle-sized bed, but that was no better.

"This bed is too soft and squishy," she mumbled. And so at last she snuggled down in the teeny-tiny bed.

"This bed is just right!" she said, and fell fast asleep.

Now, whenever there is a house with porridge and chairs and beds, there is usually someone who lives there, and that was true of this house. Three big brown bears lived there: a great big daddy bear, a middle-sized mummy bear, and a teeny-tiny baby bear.

The three bears had made their porridge and gone out for a walk in the woods while it cooled down. At last, they went home for their breakfast.

"Why is the door open?" Daddy Bear said, in his deep, gruff voice.

"Why are there footprints on the floor?" Mummy Bear said, in her soft, low voice.

Baby Bear said nothing.

They went over to the table and Daddy Bear looked in his bowl.

"Someone's been eating my porridge!" he growled.

Mummy Bear looked in her bowl.

"Someone's been eating my porridge!" she exclaimed.

Baby Bear looked in his bowl.

"Someone's been eating my porridge – and they've eaten it all up!" he cried in his teeny-tiny voice.

Daddy Bear stomped over to his chair.

"Someone's been sitting in my chair!" he growled. "There's a long hair on it!"

"Someone's been sitting in my chair!" Mummy Bear exclaimed. "The cushions are all squashed!"

Baby Bear looked at his chair.

"Someone's been sitting in my chair," he cried, "and they've broken it into pieces!"

"Let's get to the bottom of this," Daddy Bear growled, and they padded upstairs to the bedroom.

Daddy Bear saw the rumpled covers of his bed.

"Someone's been sleeping in my bed!" he grumbled.

Mummy Bear saw the jumbled pillows on her bed.

"Someone's been sleeping in my bed!" she said.

Baby Bear padded up to his bed.

"Someone's been sleeping in my bed – and they're still there!" he cried.

The three bears crowded around the sleeping girl. Baby Bear reached out a fuzzy paw to touch her golden curls.

Goldilocks opened her eyes. Imagine her surprise when she saw three bears peering down at her! She leapt out of the bed, ran down the stairs, through the door, along the path and all the way home. And she never visited the house of the three bears ever again.

The End

Pinocchio

There was once a carpenter called
Geppetto. One day, he was walking
through an enchanted forest when he heard a voice.

"Hello," it said.

Geppetto looked around, and soon realized that
the voice was coming from a magic piece of wood.

"Talking wood," he thought. "How unusual!"

Geppetto took the magic wood home and carved a
little puppet boy from it. He gave the boy a suit of clothes
and a hat with a feather in it. The wooden boy danced around the
room for Geppetto and made him laugh. "Hello!" he said.

Geppetto named the boy Pinocchio.

"You must go to school like other children," Geppetto told him.

So the next morning, Pinocchio skipped off to school on his wooden legs.

As he went along, a cricket hopped up onto his shoulder.

"You look like you could use a friend," he told Pinocchio. "I will help you to learn right from wrong."

A little further down the road, Pinocchio met a fox and a cat. They had heard the sound of dinner money jingling in his pocket.

"Don't bother going to school," said the fox. "Come and play with us instead!"

Pinocchio, not knowing any better, thought that sounded like a good idea.

"I don't think you are doing the right thing," the cricket told him. "You promised your father you would go to school."

But Pinocchio paid no attention to the cricket.

The cat and the fox led Pinocchio into a dark forest. "If you plant money here, it will grow into a money tree," they told him. "Just come back tomorrow, and you'll see."

"That doesn't sound right," said the cricket. "That money was for your dinner."

But Pinocchio didn't listen. He dug a hole in the ground and buried the coins in it.

Then Pinocchio went home, feeling very hungry. He did not tell his father that he hadn't been to school.

The next morning, Pinocchio didn't go to school either. Instead, with the cricket on his shoulder, he skipped into the forest to find his money tree.

When Pinocchio reached the spot where he'd buried his coins, there was no money tree. He dug down to look for the coins he had planted, but they were gone.

"The fox and the cat have played a trick on you," said the cricket. "They just wanted to get your money."

Pinocchio felt rather silly, but he pretended he didn't care. He stomped off into the forest.

"I'm going on an adventure," he said.

The little cricket begged him to go back to Geppetto, but Pinocchio walked on until it was dark and he was a little scared.

Soon they came to a tiny cottage. Pinocchio ran to the door and knocked loudly. A pretty fairy with turquoise hair answered the door.

"We're lost," explained Pinocchio. "Please can you help us?" The fairy invited them in and gave them some food.

"Why are you so far from home?" she asked kindly.

Pinocchio did not want to tell her that he had disobeyed his father.

"I was chased by a giant!" he lied.

Suddenly, Pinocchio's nose grew a little.

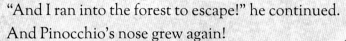

"The giant was taller than the trees…" continued Pinocchio.

Pinocchio's nose grew some more.

"And I ran into the forest to escape!" he continued.

And Pinocchio's nose grew again!

He touched it in wonder.

"I have put a spell on you!" said the fairy. "Every time you tell a lie, your wooden nose will grow."

Pinocchio began to cry. How he wished he had gone to school like his father had said!

"I won't tell any more lies," promised Pinocchio.

The fairy called some friendly woodpeckers who pecked at Pinocchio's long nose until it was back to the way it used to be.

In the morning, Pinocchio rushed back through the forest with the little cricket perched on his shoulder.

"From now on I will do just as Father tells me," he said. But when he got home, Geppetto wasn't there. Instead, there was a note on the kitchen table.

Dear Pinocchio,
I have gone to look for you. I miss you, my son.
Your loving father, Geppetto.

Pinocchio was very sad. He knew he had caused a lot of trouble.

"We must find my father and bring him home," he sobbed. So he and the cricket set off again at once.

They began their search down by the river. Pinocchio stood too near the edge of the water, and he fell in with a **SPLASH!** The cricket jumped in to help him, but they were both swallowed by an enormous fish.

There, in the fish's tummy, they found Geppetto!

Pinocchio hugged his father tightly. "I won't leave you again!" he said.

The clever wooden boy took the feather from his hat and tickled the fish.

"A... a... a... tishooo!" The fish gave a mighty sneeze and Geppetto, Pinocchio and the cricket shot back out through the fish's mouth and landed on the bank of the river.

That night, when Pinocchio was tucked up in his own little bed fast asleep, the fairy with turquoise hair flew in through his window.

"You are a good, brave boy," she said as he slept. And she kissed him on the forehead.

When Pinocchio awoke the next morning, he found that he was no longer made from wood. He was a real boy! From then on he was always a good son to Geppetto and the best of friends with the cricket, who didn't need to tell him right from wrong ever again.

The End

The Three Billy Goats Gruff

Once upon a time, there were three goats – a little white one, a medium-sized brown one and a big grey one.
They were the Billy Goats Gruff and they were brothers.
The little Billy Goat Gruff had little horns.
The medium-sized Billy Goat Gruff had medium-sized horns.
And the big Billy Goat Gruff had big, curly horns!

The three brothers lived in a small meadow beside a river. All day long they ate the green grass.

On the other side of the river, over a rickety wooden bridge, was a huge field. The Billy Goats Gruff thought the grass there looked longer and greener and juicier!

Day after day, the three Billy Goats Gruff looked longingly at the juicy grass on the other side of the river. They would have happily crossed the bridge to go there, but for one thing.

One horrible thing.

A mean and smelly old troll with very pointy teeth lived under the bridge, and he guarded it day and night.

The grass in the meadow where the three Billy Goats Gruff lived got shorter and shorter, and drier and browner, and the brothers were getting hungrier and hungrier for fresh, juicy grass.

One day, the little Billy Goat Gruff decided he'd had enough.

"I'm so hungry!" he cried to his brothers. "I can't eat one more blade of this dry, brown grass."

"We agree!" groaned his two brothers. "Look at that juicy grass over there. Oh, if only we could get past the mean old troll."

"I'm going to try," said the little Billy Goat Gruff bravely. And off he set, **TRIP TRAP, TRIP TRAP,** across the bridge.

Suddenly a croaky voice roared out, "Who's that **TRIP TRAPPING** over my bridge? I'll eat you if you pass. You'd taste yummy in a sandwich!"

"Oh, please don't eat me," cried the little goat. He was very frightened, but he had a plan. "I'm only a little goat. My brother will be crossing in a minute, and he is much bigger and tastier than me!"

The greedy troll thought about this and burped loudly. "All right," he said, "you may cross."

The little Billy Goat Gruff ran as fast as his little legs would take him until he reached the other side.

The medium-sized goat saw his little brother munching the juicy grass on the other side of the river. He really wanted to eat that grass, too.

He turned to the big Billy Goat Gruff. "If he can cross the bridge, then so can I!" he said. And off he set, **TRIP TRAP, TRIP TRAP,** across the bridge.

Suddenly, the mean troll climbed out from his hiding place.

"Who's that **TRIP TRAPPING** over my bridge? I'll eat you if you pass. You'd taste nice with rice!" He licked his lips when he noticed how much bigger this goat was.

The medium-sized Billy Goat Gruff stopped, his hooves clacking together in fear.

"Oh, please don't eat me," he cried. "I'm really not that big. My brother will be crossing in a minute, and he is so much bigger and tastier than me!"

The troll rolled his eyes, licked dribble from his chin and grunted that the medium-sized goat could cross the bridge.

The medium-sized Billy Goat Gruff galloped quickly across the bridge to join his little brother, before the mean troll changed his mind.

The big Billy Goat Gruff had been watching his brothers.

"I'm big and strong... and I'm really hungry!" he said to himself. So off he set, **TRIP TRAP, TRIP TRAP**, across the bridge to join his brothers and eat the juicy green grass on the other side.

As before, the mean, smelly troll scrabbled up onto the bridge.

"Who's that **TRIP TRAPPING** over my bridge? I'll eat you if you pass. You'd taste scrumptious in a stew!" This goat was big! The troll's mouth started watering and his large tummy started rumbling.

The big Billy Goat Gruff stamped his hooves. "No, you can't eat me!" he shouted. "I'm big and I have big horns, and I will toss you into the river if you don't let me pass."

Before the troll could answer, the big Billy Goat Gruff put his head down and charged at him. He tossed the mean creature high up into the air.

Down,
down,
down

fell the troll. With a huge splash, he dropped into the river and floated away. And that was the end of the mean troll.

"Maaaa! Well done, big brother!" laughed the little Billy Goat Gruff and the medium-sized Billy Goat Gruff. "Come and eat this grass – it is truly juicy and delicious!"

And the three Billy Goats Gruff were never hungry again.

The End

The Three Little Pigs

Once upon a time, three little pigs lived together with their mother. As they grew bigger, their small house became too crowded. So at last she sent them off into the world to seek their fortunes.

"Be careful," she said. "Here, you are safe from the big, bad wolf. But out there, you will need to build strong houses."

The pigs set off happily. After a short time, the first little pig met a farmer pulling a cartload of straw.

"Please may I have some straw to build a house?" the little pig asked.

"Certainly," the farmer said, "but it won't make a very strong house."

The little pig didn't listen. He took the bundles of straw and stacked them up to make a house. When it was finished, he went inside for a rest.

Soon, the big, bad wolf came down the road. He hadn't eaten all day. When he saw the new house of straw, his tummy rumbled and he licked his lips.

"I smell piggy," he said to himself. "Yum!"

He peeked in through the window.

"Little pig, little pig, let me come in," he growled.

"No way!" the pig shouted. "Not by the hairs on my chinny-chin-chin!"

"Well, this house doesn't look very strong," the wolf said.

"I'll huff and I'll puff, and I'll blow your house down!"

So he huffed and he puffed, and he blew the house down. Straw flew everywhere, and the little pig ran away as fast as he could.

The second little pig walked a little further. At last he came across a woodcutter with a pile of sticks.

"Please could I have some sticks to build a house?" the little pig asked.

"Certainly," said the woodcutter. "Take as many as you like, but they won't make a very strong house."

The second little pig didn't listen. He picked up all the sticks he could carry and took them to a clearing. He piled them up to make a cosy house. When it was finished, he went inside and settled down with a cup of tea.

The big, bad wolf was cross and hungry. When he saw the house of sticks, his tummy grumbled and he licked his lips.

"I smell piggy," he said to himself. "Yum, yum!"

He pushed his nose against the door.

"Little pig, little pig, let me come in," he growled.

"No way!" the second little pig shouted. "Not by the hairs on my chinny-chin-chin!"

"Well, this house doesn't look very strong," the wolf said.

"I'll huff and I'll puff, and I'll blow your house down!"

And so he huffed and he puffed, and he blew the house down. The sticks tumbled to the ground, and the little pig ran away as fast as he could.

The third little pig walked further still, until
he saw a builder with a pile of bricks. The builder
was just finishing work.

"Please could I have some bricks to build a little house?"
the third little pig asked.

"Certainly," the builder said. "Those are left over. Take
as many as you want."

So the third little pig carried the bricks away and built
a beautiful house. When he had finished, he went inside, put
a pot of water on the fire and started to make some soup.

After a while, his two brothers came running up the path.

"Let us in!" they shouted. "There's a big, bad wolf coming!"

The third little pig quickly let them in. They locked and
bolted the door and sat down to wait.

Before long, the big, bad wolf came huffing and puffing up the path. When he saw the new brick house, his tummy rumbled and grumbled and he licked his lips.

"I smell piggy – and soup!" he said to himself. "Yum, yum, yum!"

He knocked hard on the door.

"Little pig, little pig, let me come in!" he roared.

"No way!" the third little pig shouted.

"Not by the hairs on my chinny-chin-chin!"

"Well, then," the wolf said,

"I'll huff and I'll puff, and I'll blow your house down!"

And so he huffed and he puffed, and he huffed and he puffed...but the house stood firm.

The wolf looked up and saw the chimney. He climbed onto the roof, and down the chimney he went – straight into the pot of hot soup.

"Owwwooooooo!"

He jumped out of the pan and ran yowling and howling out into the cool night. The big, bad wolf ran up the path, over the hills and far away, never to be seen again. The three little pigs lived happily ever after, all together in the strong brick house.

The End

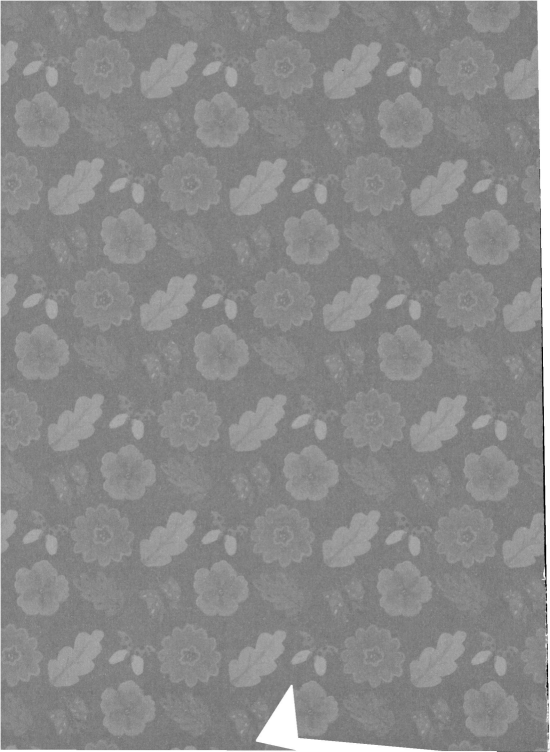